STEALING
our way
HOME

Also by Cecilia Galante
The World from Up Here

STEALING our way HOME

CECILIA GALANTE

Scholastic Press/New York

Library of Congress Cataloging-in-Publication Data

Names: Galante, Cecilia, author.
Title: Stealing our way home / Cecilia Galante.
Description: First edition. | New York : Scholastic Press, 2017. | Summary: When Pippa and Jack's mother died of cancer their world seemed to fall apart: Pippa stopped talking altogether, and Jack started picking fights, and neither of them knows how to cope with the painful and awkward sympathy from their friends and classmates—but when they learn that their father's business is failing and he is growing desperate for money they realize that there is a possibility that they will lose another parent, this time to jail.
Identifiers: LCCN 2016051620 | ISBN 9781338042962 (hardcover)
Subjects: LCSH: Bereavement—Juvenile fiction. | Brothers and sisters—Juvenile fiction. | Father and child—Juvenile fiction. | Families—Juvenile fiction. | Friendship—Juvenile fiction. | Bank robberies—Juvenile fiction. | CYAC: Grief—Fiction. | Brothers and sisters—Fiction. | Father and child—Fiction. | Family life—Fiction. | Friendship—Fiction. | Bank robberies—Fiction.
Classification: LCC PZ7.G12965 Stk 2017 | DDC 813.6 [Fic] —dc23
LC record available at https://lccn.loc.gov/2016051620

This one is for Joseph, who asked me if I was ever going to write a book about a boy.

I love you.

AUGUST

Chapter 1
PIPPA

Two weeks after Mom died, I got a letter and a book in the mail.

This is what the letter said:

Dear Pippa,

My name is Miss Rhodes, and I am going to be your fourth-grade social studies teacher next year. I am really looking forward to getting to know you and the rest of your class.

Since we will begin the fall term by learning about Greek culture, I always ask all of my students to read Tito the Warrior *(which I have enclosed) over the summer. Tito, as you will soon find out, was only a few years older than you. He lived in a part of Greece called Sparta and was raised to be a Spartan soldier. To this day, Spartans are regarded as some of the most courageous people who ever lived.*

As you read the book, please jot down at least six facts about the Spartans that you think might be important to share with the rest of the class. We'll discuss the book and go over the information you've collected during the first week of school, so please come prepared.

Have a wonderful summer, and I'll see you soon!

Sincerely,

Miss Rhonda Rhodes

I stretched out on my bed and read the letter twice, all the way through. I liked the two R's in my new teacher's name, the way they rolled over my tongue when I said them. My friend Susan can actually make a trilling sound when she says her R's, almost like she is speaking Spanish, but I've never learned how to do that.

Miss Rhonda Rhodes.

She sounded pretty. Maybe even nice. Even if she was assigning homework over the summer.

But I groaned when I picked up the book and looked at it. Definitely not my thing. The boy on the cover, who I guess was supposed to be Tito the Warrior, and which meant (at least according to Miss Rhodes) that he was just a few years older than me, looked like some weird old guy who was trying to pass as a kid. He was dressed in a long red robe and gold sandals that strapped up to his knees, and his face was all scrunched up, as if the artist had been trying to make him look fierce but instead just made him look as if he had a really bad stomachache. Plus, he was leaning forward at a weird angle, sort of crouching a little with his hands spread out in front of him, like he was about to pounce on someone or catch something. It was strange.

But who cared about school anyway? Or some dumb kid named Tito? What kind of name was Tito anyway?

Mom was gone.

Forever.

And there was nothing that anybody could do to bring her back.

I slid *Tito the Warrior* between the side of my bed and the wall. Then I crumpled the letter up into a little ball and threw it in the trash can. It bounced off the lip and rolled into the corner.

Sorry, Miss Rhonda Rhodes.

Not this year.

Not this girl.

Chapter 2
JACK

It's crazy that the whole summer has gone by and Ben and I haven't been fishing once. He called a few times to ask me to go after Mom's funeral, but I wasn't feeling it. Back then I wasn't feeling much of anything except numb, I guess. Hollow. As if all my insides had been scooped out with a giant spoon and then chucked off a cliff. Plus, the effort I knew it was going to take to dig for worms, make a bunch of sandwiches, and ride my bike to the fishing hole on the west side of the lake felt like too much. Just the thought of it kind of knocked me out. So I told him no, maybe later. After a few conversations like that, he stopped calling altogether. Before I knew it, June and July were gone, and then August, with its stifling heat and soft, swarming clouds of mosquitoes, was almost over.

But this morning, for some reason, as I woke up to the sun streaming through my window and the loons calling out on the lake, going fishing was the first thing that popped into my head. The thought of feeling that tug on the end of my line and reeling in a fish as it twisted and flopped through the water actually made me a little happy, which was something I wasn't sure I was ever going to feel again.

"Hey." I called Ben a few minutes later. "You up for some fishing today?"

No answer.

"Ben?" I wasn't sure if he'd heard me.

"Sure," he said, although he didn't sound very sure at all. "Yeah."

I leapt out of bed and raced for the shower. It'd been almost four months since I'd seen him last, which hardly seemed possible since we'd literally done just about everything together since the second grade. That was where we met, after I spotted Paul Buck making fun of Ben one day on the playground. Ben was new that year, but everyone already knew he had a stutter, that when he spoke aloud in class his face got red and his words sounded like they were being pushed through a cheese grater. That day, sitting on my swing, I could see Paul flapping his hands and spitting nonverbal sounds in Ben's direction. And for some reason, even though I didn't know the first thing about Ben, and Paul was significantly larger than me, I walked over and told Paul to stop being a jerk. I'm pretty sure it was Paul who pushed me first, and he might have even gotten my arm behind my back before I started swinging, but what I remember most about that day was how Ben wedged himself between both of us and Miss Howell and told her that it was all *his* fault, that I never would have hit anyone if he had just gone and told her what Paul was doing in the first place. We were all given twenty minutes in the Time-Out Chair in the corner of the room, but that only sealed the deal. From that day on, Ben and I were inseparable.

Now, I spot him from my bedroom window as he brakes at the edge of our driveway and leans over the handlebars. I pause for a moment, waiting for his usual "Heyyyy-oh!" greeting, but it doesn't come. Instead, he just sort of drops his chin and stares straight ahead at something down the road. His head, which his mother always shaves over the summer, is covered in peach fuzz, and even from the window, I can make out a fresh set of road burns along his left arm where the skin has been scraped off. Ever since he learned how to ride a bike, Ben has pretty much lived on anything with two wheels. He's got more scars from wrecking his bike than I probably have hairs on my head.

"Hey dog-face!" I call from the window.

Ben turns his head quickly, but he doesn't grin or say, "Takes one to know one," the way he usually does. "Hey," he says softly instead, talking to the front of my T-shirt. "You all set?" His voice sounds weird, like he's nervous. Or hiding something.

"Gimme a sec," I answer. "I just gotta grab my stuff from the garage."

He still looks the same, I think to myself as we take off down Lake Road toward the fishing hole. He's as tall and bony as he's always been, and he still has ginormous feet, which are stuck inside a pair of size eleven black LeBron James high-top sneakers. The same blue mini cooler he always brings on fishing days is strapped to the back of his bike, which, if I know Ben at all, is filled with four baloney, cheese, and yellow-mustard sandwiches, a big bag of ranch-flavored Doritos, and six cans of Sprite. But something's different. Something's off, although I can't put my finger on it yet. For one thing, he rides his bike slightly ahead of mine, instead of alongside, the way we always do. He still hasn't looked at me straight on either, as if making eye contact is suddenly weird or painful. And we go the whole half mile without saying a single word, which has never happened, not once, in all the times we've ridden down to the fishing hole. Usually we can't shut up, because the Red Sox are losing again or school stinks even more than it usually does, or Alice Jamison, who is the most annoying person on the planet, has suddenly gotten really, really pretty and neither of us knows what to do about it.

I'm the one who finally breaks the silence after we've parked our bikes and baited our lines. The sun has retreated behind a screen of clouds and the sky is a pale gray color, like wool. The best kind of fishing weather.

"So how you been?" I ask as we cast our lines into the water. "What's new?"

Ben clears his throat. "Not much. You know, same old stuff." He reels a little line in, jerks his pole over to the right.

I wonder if he realizes that how, since Mom died, nothing will ever be the same old stuff anymore, at least for me. "Whatcha been doing for the summer?" I ask.

"Mowing lawns, mostly." Ben stares at something across the lake. "My dad said I had to work, so I sort of set up a little business for myself. I have five—no, six— houses I do during the week."

"Yeah?" I straighten my shoulders a little, interested. "Is it good money?"

"Twenty-five bucks a lawn. Thirty if I have to do any extra around the edges."

"Wow, that *is* pretty good. So you're what, making like a hundred and fifty bucks a week?"

Ben nods. "More or less. My dad said I have to put half of it in the bank, but that I can do whatever I want with the other half."

"New bike?" I guess.

"You know it." The corner of his mouth lifts in a small grin, but he keeps his gaze fixed on his line. "I got my eye on a real beauty down at Sickler's. Electric orange, titanium frame, six-inch tires. I could take it all over the state if I wanted to."

"How much?"

"Three hundred and fifty."

"Ouch."

Ben grimaces. "Yeah, I know. But I only need about a hundred more bucks. Besides, I'm not in any rush. My other bike is still in pretty good shape."

I stare out at the water, wondering what it might be like to try to focus my energy on something like a job or a new bike, or anything at all for that matter. It doesn't seem possible. "Hear from anyone at school?" I ask.

"Nah, not really." He raises an eyebrow. "At least not since Field Day. Scooter Beasley ate six slices of pizza and three shaved ices, and yakked all over the rope-climbing wall. But then he nailed Mr. Lloyd in the dunk tank, so it all sort of evened out. Oh, and I won the weight-lifting contest."

"Oh yeah?" I hope Ben doesn't ask me why Pippa and I weren't there for Field Day, or why we didn't go to school at all those last few weeks. I don't know if I'd be able to explain it to him if he did, since I'm not really sure I know myself. I guess it was just a feeling of not wanting to be around anyone, maybe even ever again, although I'm not really sure why. And Dad didn't make us go. He was in such a state after Mom's funeral that I don't think he even remembered we *had* school.

"Yeah." Ben nods. "It was pretty sweet too, especially since I beat Randy Plaska. He almost popped his eyes out trying to lift the last barbell."

I smile, thinking of Randy, who is one of the biggest kids at our school and, because he likes to brag about it, one of Ben's least favorite people. "So what'd you get up to? Thirty pounds?"

Ben snorts and makes a *pfffttt* sound with his lips. "Eighty-seven. *And* straight up, over my head."

"Shut up!"

He nods, letting out some of his line, and glances a little in my direction.

"Wow." I can feel something that's been balled up tight inside start to loosen. We're getting back to where we used to be. Things will be okay. I can feel it. "Man, Ben, I'm impressed. So what else?"

"Nothing." Ben rubs the side of his nose. "You know, you guys've really been the only news."

Something zips up tight again inside when he says that, and a strange column of heat flashes down the sides of my belly. Ben looks over at me. His eyes are wide and fearful before he drops them again. "I mean . . . I didn't mean it like that, Jack. Just, you know . . . everyone's worried and stuff . . . and they still come up to me and ask for . . ."

"For what?" My voice is tight. I'm gripping the end of the pole so hard my knuckles are turning white.

"They're just checking," Ben says helplessly. "You know, to see how you are, if I've heard anything . . ."

Deep down, I know that what he's saying isn't as bad as it actually feels, that Ben's not really being a jerk and that I'm probably getting way too upset about all of it.

But right now, finding out that people have been talking about me and my family like we're the local news feels almost as bad as being at the funeral and looking up to see my entire class traipsing in behind Mr. Lloyd's bald, freckled head. Almost as bad as trying not to look at that sea of grim, somber faces as they tried to make eye contact with me and Pippa and Dad, and forcing myself not to cry. Alice Jamison was crying of course, which she had absolutely no reason to, since she'd never even met Mom. And even that felt pretty terrible, because her face was all squished up and her eyes were red and swollen. It felt like my fault, for some reason.

Suddenly, I know exactly why Ben won't look me in the eye and why he's been acting so weird. It's for the same reason I knew I couldn't go back to school those last few weeks and why I'm so furious now. He feels sorry for me. They all feel sorry for me. And everyone knows that when people start to feel sorry for you, it means they've stopped looking at you like they used to. That they probably won't ever look at you the same way again.

"That's great, Ben." I'm reeling in my line so fast I can feel the heat of it between my fingers. "I'm glad all this stuff has been such interesting *news* to all of you."

"Jack." Ben puts down his pole. "Come on, man. You know it's not like that."

"Here's what I know." I already have one leg over the seat of my bike, my pole rammed underneath the handlebars. "I know everyone in our class is a big, fat idiot. Especially you."

My front tire skids on a loose pile of gravel as I start to pedal, and I almost lose control of the bike. But at the last second, I yank it up straight and hightail it down the road.

In all the years I've known Ben, I've never called him a name, much less something as mean as a big, fat idiot.

I guess there's a first time for everything.

Chapter 3
PIPPA

The lake is the color of charcoal as I tiptoe out to the dock and sit on the edge. I love this time of the morning, when tiny slivers of pink light peek out across the water, and the soft slope of mountain behind it is draped in shadow. Pretty soon, all the dark will drain away, and the whole sky will look like the inside of a cantaloupe.

I peer carefully at the trees along the shoreline and even stand up so I can see inside the cluster of cattails bunched up to the right of the dock, but there's still no sign of Mr. Thurber. Where could he be? This is the first summer I can remember that he's been gone more than he's been here. Usually, he'll perch in the willow tree in back of our next-door neighbor Nibs' house and preen his feathers with his long, yellow beak. Sometimes he'll watch me when I sit down on the dock, and he'll tip his head, like he's about to ask me a question. And then, without warning, he'll spread his great white wings and lift himself out of the tree gliding across the water like a long, thin airplane. Those are the times I like best, when he's flying. When he's part of the sky and the water, all at the same time. It makes me feel safe for some reason, watching him. Like everything's the way it's supposed to be. Like nothing else can go wrong.

"Is that you, Pippa?" Nibs is standing in a yellow square of light just inside her kitchen door, still in her bathrobe and slippers. I raise my hand and wave. "How about a chai?" she whispers loudly. I nod yes. "Blueberry?" I nod a second time. "All right. Give me five minutes." She disappears inside the house again.

Nibs has lived next to us on the lake for as long as I can remember. She is famous for her garden and her chai lattes. She drinks at least four of them every day and adds in all different kinds of flavors. One time she even put a little jalapeño pepper in a batch, but it didn't go over very well. My favorite is the blueberry, which is not too sweet and tastes a little like licorice. Nibs likes cinnamon.

I pull Mom's pink sweater down over my knees and look out over the water again. The surface is smooth as glass and just as still. Mom's sweater has white buttons in the front and deep pockets. She wore it in the hospital during the very last week, and now I wear it every morning when I come out here. I put my head down against the soft material and inhale. Lilacs. Wrigley's Doublemint gum. Cough syrup. For some reason, the smell of her doesn't make me cry this morning. Does that mean I'm starting to miss her less? I can't even imagine such a thing. Most days, I miss her in a way that I didn't know I could ever miss someone. I don't wake up crying anymore, but lots of times during the day, I'll think about her and something will start to hurt in the back of my throat. I have to keep swallowing to make it go away, and sometimes even that doesn't work.

Nibs' footsteps sound on the dock behind me. She's changed out of her bathrobe and slippers into her denim overalls and heavy work boots. Her usual strand of pearls dangles around her neck, small and delicate in the pale light, and the morning newspaper is tucked under one arm. Nibs is a serious newspaper reader. Sometimes in the morning she'll just sit here and read while I watch for Mr. Thurber.

"Here you are," she says, handing me one of the mugs. "I added extra foam at the top, the way you like it." She sits down heavily next to me, the dock groaning under her weight. Nibs told me once that she was built like a man, with big shoulders and legs, but I think she looks very much like a lady.

I smile my thanks and take a sip. The chai is perfect: creamy, sweet, and best of all, warm.

"Sleep well?" Nibs asks, crossing her legs in a vague sort of pretzel shape. I nod, although it's not the truth. I woke up sweating after another nightmare about Mom.

This one had water and a big black box in it. "Good. Me too." Nibs sighs deeply. "There is nothing in the whole wide world as lovely as a good night's sleep. It can change your whole outlook on life, you know that?"

I stare out at the water. Blink a few times.

"You didn't sleep well, did you?" Nibs asks softly.

My eyes fill with tears, which I don't understand. Is it because of the nightmare, or because sometimes, like right now, Nibs' way of knowing something about me without me having to say anything reminds me so much of Mom that it makes me want to run as fast as possible in the opposite direction? I shrug, wiping at my eyes with the back of Mom's sweater sleeve.

"Bad dream?" Nibs asks.

I nod.

She puts an arm around my shoulder. For a few minutes, we just sit there, not saying anything. But she doesn't have to. Her arm, which is the perfect weight, is enough.

Behind us, a car trundles by on the dirt road beyond our house. Gravel crunches beneath the tires, and the head-lights are long and yellow. After another minute, they fade away. The crack of pink light on the other side of the lake is getting bigger. Wider. Pretty soon, it will burst open, and the color will slip from cantaloupe to watermelon.

"Any sign of Mr. Thurber?" Nibs asks.

I shake my head and stir the top of my chai foam with the tip of my finger. It feels like a cloud.

"I bet he got himself a girlfriend," Nibs says. "That's what I think. He went and found himself a pretty little girl heron with fantastic legs."

I smile a little.

Nibs shrugs. "It happens, you know? Even with great white herons. They meet, fall in love, start spending time at each other's places. He's probably over at her pad right now, sprucing everything up. Then, when he's finished, he'll want to bring her here. I bet we'll see both of them any day now." She points to the willow tree. "Right up there, just like always."

My smile gets bigger. I hope she's right.

Nibs takes a big gulp of her chai, cupping the mug with her broad hands. "You know what I like best about living on the lake?"

I look up at her, waiting. Nibs is a whole lot older than Mom was, but she doesn't have very many wrinkles. Mom used to rub a rose-scented cream all over her face every night before she went to bed. I wonder if Nibs does the same thing.

"How much it surprises you." She nods, as if agreeing with herself. "Every day. When you least expect it."

I remember the first time Mom told me about Nibs. How much it surprised me when she said Nibs was an art teacher at the high school in Poultney. She didn't look like any schoolteacher I'd ever known. She looked like a farmer. Or a truck driver. With pearls.

"You looking forward to going back to school?" Nibs asks.

I shake my head. I'll be starting fourth grade, and I'm dreading it.

"Me either," Nibs says. "Lucky for you, the elementary school doesn't start until Wednesday. High school starts on Monday." She sighs. "It always comes around too soon, doesn't it? I never feel ready to go back. Like I haven't wrung everything out of summer quite yet."

I nod in agreement.

"You'll have some new teachers," Nibs says carefully. "They'll probably want you to talk every once in a while."

I bite my bottom lip, swing my legs under the dock. I haven't talked in a long time. Not since Mom died.

Nibs pulls something out of the front pocket of her overalls. "Of course, you might have a real nice teacher this year who'll let you write your answers instead of speaking them." She places a palm-sized notebook into my lap. It's pink, which is my favorite color, and sprinkled with tiny white polka dots. "You could use that for a while if you want. Write out your answers, maybe?" She puts a hand on the back of my head, smoothing my hair down with her palm. "I have a few friends over at the elementary school, Pippa. I hope it's okay that I went in and talked to them about what's been going on with you. Filled them in a little."

I lean into her, hoping she can feel how grateful I am. She smells like milk and cinnamon and pipe smoke. I close my eyes as a slight breeze caresses my face. Pretend, just for a moment, that it is Mom, whispering good morning.

Even though I know better.

Chapter 4
JACK

I'm trying to get the TV to work the next morning when Dad comes out of the bathroom dressed in boxer shorts and a T-shirt. A big gob of shaving cream is smeared along his neck, and he's rubbing the back of his hair with a towel. I rattle the clicker again and start taking out the batteries.

"Don't bother," Dad says, sinking down next to me on the couch. "Electric's out."

"What do you mean, it's out?"

"I mean it's out." There's an edge to his voice as he leans forward and rubs his head again. "I got a notice in the mail yesterday. They turned it off this morning. It's out."

"Why'd they turn it off?"

"Why do you think they turned it off, Jack?" He turns on me angrily, his face a map of lines. "Because I'm behind on the bill, okay? That's what happens in this country when you miss a few payments. They penalize you. Take things away. I'll get it fixed, all right? I'm on it."

I bite my lower lip, stare at the gray screen in front of us. The inside of my nose is tingling. I reach up and pinch it hard. It seems like anything these days can bring these idiot feelings up, but there's no way I'm going to cry. No freaking way. Not in front of Dad. And not about something as stupid as the electric bill. I stand up instead and stride across the room.

"Jack."

"*What?*"

"Don't go, okay? Please." He hangs his head for a moment and then lifts it again. "I'm sorry."

I turn back around, flick my eyes over him. He looks so tired. His hair has gotten even grayer around the ears, and the circles under his eyes, which appeared like pale little crescent moons right after we first heard the news about Mom, look even deeper. Darker. "You didn't have to yell at me." My voice is softer. "I just didn't know."

"I know." Dad pats the empty spot on the couch. "It's not your fault. I'll take care of it. Don't worry. Come on, sit back down a minute. Tell me how things are going."

I plop back down, cross my arms over my chest. "I didn't even hear you come in last night."

"I got caught up with some things at the office again. It was pretty late."

I stare straight ahead, watching the wall blur in front of me. Ever since Mom got sick, Dad's been completely

22

obsessed with "some things at the office." Most nights, he doesn't even get home from the car dealership until nine o'clock. I can't remember the last time the three of us had dinner together. Or the last time it wasn't hot dogs.

"So, what's been going on around here?" he asks amiably. "What'd you do yesterday?"

I shrug. Push down a thought about Ben. "Not a lot."

"Nothing at all?"

"Worked on the tree house. Cut the grass. Went fishing with Ben."

"You went fishing?" Dad sticks one end of the towel inside his ear and starts rubbing again. "Did you take Pippa with you?"

"She was hanging out with Nibs."

"Oh yeah? What were they doing?"

"Working in the garden. Like always."

Dad smiles faintly and looks at something across the room. "Good ol' Nibs," he says softly.

I can hear the gratitude in his voice. I know he feels good that someone like Nibs lives next door. Especially now. Not only is she a responsible adult, but Nibs has always been good to Pippa, right from the beginning. Her real name is Mrs. Nivens, but Pippa, who couldn't pronounce it when she was little, started calling her Nibs and it stuck. Now we all call her Nibs, even Dad. She's a nice enough lady, I guess, but honestly, I think she's a little weird. And not just because she's old and is constantly digging in the dirt. She smokes a pipe, too. And two of her teeth are yellow, right in the front. Plus, I've never in my whole life seen her without the same string of pearls around her neck. Even when she's wearing overalls and work boots. I don't know what it is, really, but there's something about her that's just a little bit . . . off.

"What about you guys?" Dad asks. "You catch any fish?"

"Nah. We were only there a half hour."

"Not biting, huh?"

"I guess."

"Been pretty hot," Dad says. "Even early in the morning."

"Yeah."

"You and Ben come back here, then?"

"No, he left. I went up to the tree house. Got to listen to Nibs talk Pippa's ear off all afternoon."

Dad chuckles. "What was she talking about this time?"

"Her plants. The weather. Oh, and something about Mr. Thurber."

"Mr. Thurber?" Dad repeats. "Why? Did something happen to him?"

"No, they just haven't seen him in a few days, I guess. I doubt it's anything. He's probably just hanging around some other part of the lake."

Mr. Thurber, who is a great white heron, is practically part of the family. Mom found him on the side of the road on her way to work one day even before Pippa or

I were born. He'd been hit by a car and was almost dead, but Mom brought him back to the house and nursed him back to health. Ever since then, except in the winter when he flies down south, Mr. Thurber comes to the edge of the dock every morning and stands there until one of us waves hello. I swear he thinks he knows us. Or at least that we know him.

Dad rubs the inside of his other ear and then sighs. "Pippa didn't say anything, did she?"

"Nope." I stare at the gray television screen again, feel something inside close like a door. Dad asks me the same question every day, but Pippa hasn't talked in over four months, not since the last day at the hospital. I know Dad blames me. We had a fight that day, Pippa and me, right outside Mom's hospital room, and I told her to shut up. Actually, I told her that she'd been talking so much and asking so many dumb questions that she'd probably worn Mom out, which was why the nurse asked us finally to leave the room and let her rest. That was when I told her that if she didn't learn to shut up for once in her life, she was going to wear me out, too.

A half hour later, Mom was dead.

Pippa hasn't said a word since.

"Listen," Dad says, "I have some really important meetings today, so I'm going to need you to take Pippa downtown to get some new school clothes. For you too, obviously. Neither of you can start school next week in your old summer stuff."

"Wait, you want *me* to take her?"

"Yeah, if you would. I can't do it right now. I told you, I have these meetings."

"Dad, *I* don't know what kind of clothes to get her. I don't even know what size she is! Can't you just take her this weekend?"

"More meetings," Dad says. "Saturday and Sunday. I'm sorry, Jack. I know I'm dropping the ball right now, but I've got a few things lined up that are looking good." He looks straight at me. "Really good."

Having things "lined up" is another thing I've learned not to press too hard about. Last month, it was some wacky get-rich-quick scheme that Dad fell for, buying five thousand boxes of blue vitamins that a guy from San Diego convinced him to invest in and then sell. Apparently, it could cure everything, from headaches to cancer. Yeah, right. The only thing it "cured" was Dad's lopsided bed after he shoved a few of the vitamin boxes under it to level it out.

"Okay, whatever." I hope Dad can hear the aggravation in my voice. "But I'm telling you, I have no idea what kind of clothes she likes. Especially nice ones for school."

"Let her pick out whatever she wants," Dad says practically. "Within reason, of course. No belly shirts or anything. Nothing with heels. How about you? What do you need?"

What do I need? Is he kidding? I need him to come home before nine o'clock every night. I need Ben to show up on his bike and ask me to go fishing again. I need Mom to walk into the living room right now wearing her light purple robe and holding her favorite coffee cup, with the chip on the handle, that Pippa made her in kindergarten. "Some new jeans," I say instead. "A few shirts."

"Good, good. Get some shoes, too. Boots, sneakers, whatever. And underwear." He takes out his wallet from his back pocket and pulls out a credit card. "Just give them this."

"They'll let me use it?" I hold the card between my thumb and index finger, studying the long series of inverted numbers along the front. "Without you there?"

"Oh, please." Dad waves off my concern. "Money is money. Stores will take anything from anybody as long as it's legit." And then, noticing the hesitation on my face, he says, "Just call me if there's a problem. I'll talk to them and make sure they know the card is mine."

"Okay." I slide the card into my pocket. "If you say so."

"I say so." Dad stands up again, holding both ends of the wet towel. "And don't worry so much all the time, okay, buddy?" He reaches out and ruffles my hair with his fingers. "Everything's fine. It really is."

I stare at the TV screen for a long time after he leaves the room. The truth is I don't even care that it doesn't work. I'd rather be outside reinforcing the floor on my tree house than sitting in front of the TV anyway. But I do care *why* it doesn't work. For some reason, Dad has money to buy us new school clothes right now, but not to pay the electric company. When she was alive, Mom was the one who took care of all the financial stuff. She used to have a piece of paper taped to the inside of the cereal cupboard in the kitchen that listed all the bills and when they had to be paid. Every time she paid one, she would put a check mark next to it. By the time the month had ended, the sheet was filled with check marks, and we'd all do something fun, like go to the movies or out to dinner with the money she had left over. It wasn't like we were ever rich—not even close—but the way Mom did things, and with her close attention to detail, we never had to worry either. Which, when I think about it now, was like being rich in a whole other way.

Now that she's gone though, the whole money situation has been turned upside down. Dad's not the type to tape a list to the inside of the cereal cupboard; he's more the kind of guy who throws the bills into a drawer and then starts panicking when he can't find them again. And I can't remember when—or if—there's ever been any extra money at the end of the month.

You wouldn't think I'd know about the money part, being only twelve and all. Maybe I wouldn't if Dad didn't feel the need to tell me everything now. Which he does. Especially late at night, after a few beers. That's how I know that the blue vitamin project was just a scam. And that he lost every last penny in his savings account because of it. And that the bank is breathing down his neck about payments on the house because he hasn't sold a car in over six months.

That's how I know that things have gone from bad to worse.

And that if I don't figure out a way to help him out pretty soon, it might get even worse than that.

Chapter 5
PIPPA

The sun is all the way out now, big and round in the sky, and the view across the lake is so clear I can see individual trees along the tops of the mountains. The water shimmers like wet silver, the surface of it smooth and gray. Nibs went back inside at least an hour ago, taking her mugs with her, but I haven't moved. She left the paper for me, the way she always does, so that I can read the funny pages, but I haven't looked at it yet. I'm hoping that if I sit very, very still and breathe very, very quietly, Mr. Thurber will come out from wherever he is hiding. Because he must be hiding. Maybe he's trying to play a trick on us. Or he thinks he's being funny. Except that everyone knows jokes stop being funny when they last this long.

"Pippa?" Dad calls from the back door suddenly. "Honey, I'm heading out to work!"

I get up quickly and run to him. Dad catches me in a bear hug, squeezing tight, and then lets go, stepping back a little so that he can see my face.

"I'm so sorry I missed dinner again last night." He tucks a piece of hair behind my ear. "I had to work late."

I nod, fiddling with the small white button on the cuff of his shirt.

"Jack said he made hot dogs. Any good?"

I shrug, inserting the button back in its hole.

"Any sign of Mr. Thurber yet?"

I shake my head, tracing the thin leather band of his watch. I want to tell him about the conversation I just had with Nibs. Especially the part about the little pink notebook. And her going to talk to my teacher. How I feel a little bit better because of it, that maybe things won't be so awful when I have to go back to school after all. I want to tell him that wearing Mom's sweater makes me feel warm and sad all at the same time. And I want to tell him that Jack's hot dogs were the worst thing I've ever eaten in my life—shriveled, rubbery, and cold in the middle. But I can't do it yet. I just can't.

Dad sighs. "I'm sure he'll come around. Herons are persnickety little buggers. They get attitudes. Think they can go anywhere and do anything they want."

He reaches under my chin and tilts it up. A funny look comes over his face as he brushes my bangs to one side. It makes me feel embarrassed. I close my eyes, try to duck out from under his gaze.

"Wow, Pip, you look older, you know that?"

I blink a little, lower my face even more.

He traces a fingertip along the edge of my hairline. "All this baby stuff is gone. You look a little bit more serious. Mature." He pauses, grins. "You're how old now?"

I hold up ten fingers.

"My double-digit girl," he says softly. "That must be it. Yesterday you were three, and now you're almost a teenager. You're growing up, sweetheart." He hugs me again, and when he does, wrapping both of his arms around my shoulders and bending over to kiss the top of my head, I wish that I could ask him to come home early tonight. That the nights he comes home so late are always the nights I have the terrible nightmares about Mom.

But he lets go too fast, and just as I start to feel something move in the back of my throat, he's gone again.

The microwave won't work. I push all the right buttons, open and shut the door, even unplug the thick cord in the back and plug it back into the wall again. But the little screen stays dark. None of the green buttons on the side light up either. How am I supposed to make my apple-cinnamon oatmeal?

Jack comes in, scratching his head. His hair has gotten long and shaggy over the last couple of months, and his shorts and T-shirt, which he probably slept in, are a mass of wrinkles.

"The electricity's out," he says, his voice thick with

sleep. "You're gonna have to eat something else for breakfast." He goes to the fridge, takes out a half gallon of chocolate milk, and brings the container to his lips.

I watch his Adam's apple bob up and down as he swallows, Mom's voice ringing in my ear: "You put that carton down, Mr. Manners, and get yourself a glass."

Suddenly, a strange look comes over his face as he rushes to the sink and spits out the milk. "Bleechhhh! It's sour!" He wipes his mouth with the back of his hand and opens the refrigerator again. It's dark inside. "No refrigerator, either." His shoulders slump as he walks over to the window and stares out at the lake.

Why is the electricity out? Why doesn't the refrigerator work? I wait for Jack to explain, but he just stands there, looking out the window. I take my bowl out of the microwave and stir the flakes of oatmeal. Maybe I'll just eat it dry. It can't be that bad, can it?

"Who's that girl on the Andersons' dock?" Jack asks suddenly.

I swing my bare feet under the table and take a bite of the oatmeal. It tastes like little bits of paper, and I spit it back out.

"You see her?" Jack asks. I pick out one of the dried pieces of apple and nibble the edge of it. If he'd said something about Mr. Thurber, I would have leapt out of my seat. I don't really care too much about other girls. Except for Nibs.

"C'mere. Pippa. Look, will you?"

I get out of my seat and glance out the window. Some girl is sitting on the Andersons' dock, on the other side of Nibs' house, with her legs draped over the edge. Her hair is so long that it hangs down around both sides of her face like curtains. It's hard to tell from here, but it looks like she's wearing pink cowboy boots.

"Have you ever seen her before?" Jack asks.

I shrug.

"Is that a yes or a no?"

I shake my head no and head back over to the table.

Jack turns around again. He doesn't say anything for a long time. I know he's probably thinking she's pretty and that maybe he'll work up the nerve to go say hi to her. Except that Jack would never do anything like that. The only thing that scares him more than pretty girls is the thought of actually having to talk to one.

I get up from the table and grab one of Nibs' newspapers, which I keep in a pile next to the sink. It's an old one from two weeks ago, but I don't care. This morning's paper is still on the dock, and I need something to read while I eat.

"Listen, Pippa." Jack walks over to the table and leans against a chair. "You and me have to go into town today and get some new clothes for school." He opens a bag of white bread and takes out the last four slices.

34

I slump down against one arm. I hate shopping about as much as I hate dry oatmeal. Which, looking down into my still-full bowl, is saying something.

"Yeah, well, I feel the same way." Jack shoves bread into his mouth. "But Dad gave me his credit card and said we have to go. He said you could pick out whatever you want. As long as it's not a belly shirt or anything with heels."

I roll my eyes. Like I'd ever wear a belly shirt.

Jack crams the last of the bread into his mouth and looks up at the clock. "It's only nine o'clock now. The stores don't even open 'til ten. We have lots of time. I'm gonna ride down to the junkyard to look for some more wood for the tree house. You go upstairs and get ready. When I get back, we'll go, all right?"

Junkyard, my foot. Jack's already got more wood stacked up in the backyard than he can use in a year. He's going to Finster's Rock, just around the bend in the lake, so he can stare at that girl without her knowing.

The house is so quiet after he leaves that I almost start to cry. I like the quiet outside, with the stillness of the water and the silence of the sun, but inside, all it does is scare me. It's funny how the sound of nothing can be filled with so much something. Whatever something is.

I turn my attention back to the newspaper and read the funny pages. But none of them are funny, so I start leafing through the middle section. Most of the stories, which seem to be about church festivals and something called stock inflations, are boring. Like, *really* boring. I'm not really sure what Nibs always seems so worked up about when it comes to reading this thing. She pores over it from front to back every morning, as if someone's hidden something in there that she's got to find.

Finally, on the third page, there is a story that catches my attention. It's about a man who put on a Spider-Man mask and walked into a bank. He handed the lady behind the counter a note that said he had a gun and that he would use it if she didn't give him all the money in her register. But the lady started to cry, and when another bank person came over to help her, the man got scared and ran out.

I shake my head, rereading the last part again about him running out. What a dope. Then again, if you're dumb enough to rob a bank wearing a Spider-Man mask, I guess you'd be dumb enough to run back out again without any money.

On the other side of the Spider-Man story is an article about a curly-haired lady who caught a forty-five-pound catfish in Lake Bomoseen. I lean in so I can examine the fish up close. Catfish are ugly, and this one is no exception. Its long whiskers hang down near the woman's knees, and its eyes are as big as pool balls. **WHAT A WHOPPER!** says the headline. The lady, who is wearing a big orange windbreaker and a blue knit hat, is smiling so hard it looks like her face might break in half. I can't really blame her.

Jack will be so jealous. The biggest fish he ever caught weighed six pounds and was about as long as his arm. But then, he's never been much of a fisherman.

I cut out the picture and hang it on the refrigerator. Jack'll spit when he sees it.

Chapter 6
JACK

The girl is still there when I crawl out on the ledge of Finster's Rock and peek over. Finster's Rock isn't so much a rock as it is a kind of packed dirt cliff with a ledge, but everyone's always called it that anyway. It's just around the bend from the Andersons' place, with a perfect bird's-eye view of the Andersons' dock, so it's the absolute best place to be. When I catch sight of her, my heart does a belly flop in the middle of my chest. The surface of the ledge is so hot that I have to balance myself on the inside of my wrists and then scooch all the way over to the left side, where there's a tiny bit of shade. But it's worth it.

Man, is it worth it.

She's sitting on the end of the dock just like before, except that now her face is tilted up, like she's trying to get some sun. Her neck is as long and thin as a reed. It's hard to know how old she is from this distance, but she is without a doubt the most beautiful girl I've ever seen. Even prettier than Alice Jamison, which is really saying something. This girl's got light brown hair that spills down over her shoulders, a little nose, and a round chin. Her jean shorts are frayed at the bottom and the green T-shirt she's wearing has something I can't make out written on the front. Her long, brown legs disappear inside a pair of pink cowboy boots, and she's crossed one ankle over the other.

Who *is* she? And why is she sitting on the Andersons' dock? I wonder if they are related. Mr. and Mrs. Anderson are definitely old enough to be her parents, but they just got married a few years ago. She can't be their daughter. Maybe she's a niece. Or a friend of the family. But what's she doing here on the lake? And how long will she be around?

I watch, spellbound, as she stands up suddenly and stretches, reaching up toward the sky with both hands. Her pink boots go up almost to her knees and I can only make out a single word—HAT—in the middle of her shirt. Hat? Hat what?

I try to imagine what her name might be. Jennifer? Samantha? Lindsey? Maybe she has a really unusual name. Something different like Ainsley or Thora that sounds like music and makes you think of the woods or whole other countries. But this girl doesn't look like a Thora. Or an Ainsely. She looks more like a Rose. Or a Summer.

I watch as she reaches around the back of her jean shorts and pulls out a small package that could be a deck of cards or a pack of gum. She reaches inside the package, pulls something out with her thumb and forefinger, and inserts it into her mouth. She chews for a few moments and then, puckering her lips, leans forward and spits. It's impossible to know from this distance what has traveled from her mouth into the water, but the long, smooth arc of it, combined with the distance it travels, are equally mind-blowing. I sit still as a deer as the girl chews and spits another four times. All of them travel just as far—if not farther—than the first, each one suspended over the water in a single, fluid curve before dropping into it again with a tiny plop. The ripples in the water spread out like butter melting and then fade away into nothing.

She's the best spitter I've ever seen, boy or girl. And I know without a doubt that by the time she turns and walks back into the house, I'm halfway crazy in love.

"Pippa!" I yell, braking so hard in the driveway that the dust curls up in big clouds around my legs. "You ready?" Pippa's face appears in the upstairs window. "Come on, let's go!"

I head over to the garage to pull out her bike. It's pink, with a glittery banana seat and long, white streamers. She's only ridden it once or twice since Mom got sick, but she has to ride it today. Downtown Poultney is three miles from the lake, and there's no way I'm walking. Especially afterward, when we'll be armed with bags of clothes looped over the handlebars. The bike makes a strange clinking sound as I roll it out, and I squat down to take a look. The chain is off the track. Again. Dad said he'd get it fixed the last time Pippa rode it, but he never did. No surprise there. Work is the only thing he ever has time for anymore.

Pippa comes out and stands next to me, watching silently as I fiddle with the chain. "It fell off again," I say, trying to guess what she might be thinking. "I'm just getting it back on the track. I'll be done in a second."

She nudges my shoulder with something until I look up. It's a little pink notebook, the kind you can fit in your pocket, with wire loops at the top. She's written something on one of the pages. I lean forward, reading the words. "Did you find any wood?"

I look up at her. The question isn't coming from her mouth, but it's still a question. It's still a way of speaking. For the first time in four months. The inside of my nose tingles. I want to shout. I want to reach out and hug her. Tell her thank you for not staying inside there, where it's so dark and sad all the time. Thank her for coming out here. Even if she's just peeking her nose out. Even if it's just for a little bit.

Instead, I pinch my nose. Rub the little space beneath it with the edge of my finger. "No, there wasn't much there today," I answer. And then, "Where'd you get that notebook?"

She writes something carefully with her pink glitter pen and then turns the notebook around again. "Nibs."

I nod, smiling a little to myself.

Good old Nibs.

Pearls or no pearls, she's a pretty good egg.

Chapter 7
PIPPA

I have to focus on pedaling. I haven't been on my bike in a long time and it feels a little wobbly. Lake Road is bumpy and pebbly, too, which makes it feel like I'm going to fall. We'll only be on this road for about ten minutes, though. After that, we'll switch over to Route 30, which is straight, smooth pavement all the way into Poultney.

The sun is high overhead now, and it feels good against my bare arms. The smell of green is everywhere. Wild blackberry bushes clot the edge of the road. Their branches are heavy with berries as big as my nose. My stomach growls just looking at them. That dry, cold oatmeal didn't do a thing. I'm starving.

"So I thought we'd just go to Murphy's," Jack says, looking over his shoulder. "They'll have all the clothes we need, plus shoes. And they take credit cards."

I nod, gripping my handlebars. Murphy's is as good a store as any, I guess. Mom used to take us there every year when it was time for back-to-school shopping. But that was just the beginning. After Murphy's, we'd have to go to a couple of stores at the mall in Middletown Springs for shoes and underwear, and then to Kmart and Target in Rutland for school supplies. It was a long, long day.

"You want to start with a milk shake at Dipsy Do's?" Jack asks. "Like Mom used to?"

I nod happily. Sometimes I wonder if Jack and I think about the same things when it comes to Mom. Or maybe it's just that he's a lot like her. He even looks like she did. Dark hair. Lots of freckles across the bridge of his nose. Little, sort-of-pointed ears. He's built like she was too, with superlong legs and arms and hardly any neck. I look more like Dad, with my paler skin and green eyes, although I'm the only one with red hair, which I used to hate until I read *Pippi Longstocking* last year. Now I kind of like it. Dad says my red hair fits my personality. It might be the only thing that does anymore.

"I can't believe we have to go back to school next week," Jack calls from up ahead. He slows down a little so that I can catch up to him. "You excited for fourth grade?"

I shake my head. I honestly can't imagine anything worse right now than having to go back to school. I know the kids will look at me funny the way they all do after something bad happens to someone. They looked at Marissa Shedlock that way last year after her dad made a scene at the Christmas pageant and yelled a bad word at her mom. Being looked at because I don't have a mom anymore might be worse than having a mom who gets things yelled at her, but I don't really know, because Dad never yelled anything at Mom, not ever. Even Molly and Susan, who used to sit with me at lunch, will look at me different, and I don't want them to. I don't want them to look at me at all.

"Yeah, me either," Jack says glumly. "Although Ben told me last year that seventh grade is supposed pretty cool." He pauses, pushing down hard on his pedals. "I just don't know if I want to see anyone yet. Or answer anybody's questions."

I nod.

I think Jack and I think about *exactly* the same things when it comes to Mom. And maybe a lot of other things, too.

The inside of Dipsy Do's is white and cool. Ceiling fans whir softly overhead, and the white wicker furniture has new blue-checkered seats.

"Hi there!" A tall, thin man with blond hair and wire glasses leans over the counter. "What can I help you with?"

By the look on Jack's face, I can tell that he's never seen the blond man before either.

"Where's Mr. Switzer?" Jack asks.

"Oh, he's on vacation," the man says. "He flew to Alaska on Tuesday to do some salmon fishing. I'm just looking after things until he gets back."

"Oh." Jack is as disappointed as I am. Mr. Switzer is the owner of Dipsy Do's. He reminds me of Santa Claus, with his big belly and long, white beard. I can't remember the last time we came for ice cream and he wasn't here, pulling at the end of his white whiskers and telling us funny jokes. It feels strange that he's gone, even if it's just on vacation. Like something else is off.

Jack and I sit at the counter toward the back and order our milk shakes from the new guy. Double-chocolate for Jack, coffee-vanilla for me. Just like we used to. Mom always ordered strawberry, topped with three big swirls of whipped cream and a cherry, which she would save until the very last bite.

"Enjoy!" the man says brightly, sliding Jack's shake in front of him. "I'll be up front if you need me."

Jack and I clink our glasses together, bend our heads over our straws, and take a long sip. But then the weirdest thing happens. As soon as the cold ice cream fills my mouth, my throat tightens and this strange sensation comes over me. It's like Mom's *in* the milk shake. Or at least remembering her is. For a split second she's right there on the empty stool between us, her long legs tucked around the bottom of it, her eyes getting real round as she pulls hard on the straw, looks sideways at me and then over Jack, until we all start laughing.

I swallow as hard as I can, forcing the liquid over an acorn-sized knot and wince in pain. Tears fill my eyes. I bend over the straw again, pretending to sip, not wanting Jack to see me. But when I peek over at him, he's stopped drinking his, too. He's just stirring it with one hand and wiggling his nose. I pull on his shirt. Point to my milk shake and shake my head.

"Come on," he says, tilting his head toward the door. "It's okay. We don't have to finish them."

It's hot outside. For a moment, both of us stand on the front step of Dipsy Do's and blink under the sun. "You okay?" Jack asks after a minute.

I nod.

"Dumb idea." He takes a deep, deep breath and lets it out. "Come on. We have clothes to buy anyway."

I stay as close to Jack as he'll let me as we walk our bikes down the sidewalk. There are a few people walking down Main Street, drinking coffee and talking on their phones. It makes me think about the man I saw on the day of Mom's funeral. The one with the hot dog.

We were all in the cemetery, standing around silently as her coffin was being lowered into the ground. I didn't want to watch, because it scared me, thinking about her long arms and legs and all the muscles and bones inside of them being so deep underground, beneath all that dirt, so I closed my eyes. When I opened them again, I saw a man across the street eating a hot dog. He was actually walking very fast and eating a hot dog, as if maybe he was on his lunch break and was late getting back to work. I remember thinking how strange it was that he was just walking along and eating a hot dog while my mother was being lowered in the ground underneath all that dirt. It didn't make any sense to me at all. But then, that was how everything felt back then. Like it had been turned upside down. Inside out. As if it might never make sense again.

"Pippa?" Jack turns around as Murphy's comes into view and grabs my hand. "Come on, now. Let's get this over with, okay?"

His hand feels warm in mine.

I tighten my fingers around it so that he can't let go.

Chapter 8
JACK

Man, I miss her.

Sometimes, just before I get to the front door of the house, I'll forget that she's not here anymore, and as I turn the knob and push it open, it's like nothing ever happened. Like everything is back to the way it was, all warm and yellow, Mom in her chair by the kitchen window, her hair pinned up on top of her head, rummaging through a cookbook for dinner ideas. She used to look up as soon as I'd come in from school and her whole face would break into a smile. "There's my guy!" she'd say. "What can I get you before you climb up into that tree of yours?"

And then I see her chair.

And the empty spot by the window.

And it's just like what I felt at that stupid ice-cream place, drinking the same exact milk shake I used to order every time she took us shopping for school clothes. Like the inside of my stomach has dropped out. Like everything around me has stopped. And then shuddered.

49

Usually when that happens, I turn back around, head out to the tree house, and pound nails into the wood until my arm feels like it's going to fall off. Today though, I'm not anywhere near the tree house. So instead, I'm going to do what Dad keeps doing and push through it.

I hold Pippa's hand tight as I lead her over to the girls' section at Murphy's. She's a little shaken up from the ice-cream place too, which makes me feel terrible since it was my idea, so I make a big deal of pointing out how nice everything looks on the racks. I even pull out some outfits, which is what Mom used to do, and try to get her interested.

"Remember, Dad said whatever you want." I hold up a peach blouse with white ruffles down the front. It's a nice color, but it looks gigantic next to her. The tag around the collar says 14/16. "Actually, this looks too big," I say, putting it back on the rack. "Do you know what size stuff you wear now?"

Pippa shakes her head no and stares dumbly at the clothes. She's still holding my other hand. I don't have the heart to shake her off. I just hope no one I know walks in here and sees us. "Lemme look at the back of your T-shirt," I say, yanking the neck part of her shirt out so I can check the size. "See, I was right. This says 8/10. Let's go over here to the smaller sizes."

There is a silver rounder in the corner with smaller-looking girls' clothes. I pull out a pant-and-shirt combo that says size 10. "How about this one?" It's pink with little blue flowers on the front. A tiny bow in the middle. "The pants match, and they're nice and soft," I say encouragingly. "They'll be real easy to pull on."

Pippa stares at it again and then nods slowly. I almost shout I'm so relieved. Maybe this won't be so terrible after all. The remembering or the shopping.

We go through the same routine—me holding the clothes up, Pippa nodding or shaking her head—until she has approved at least six new outfits.

"All right," I say finally. "I think that's probably good for now, unless you see something else you like. Do you want to go downstairs to the dressing rooms and try everything on?"

Pippa shakes her head.

I hesitate, wondering if I should force her, and then change my mind. Trying on clothes every year when we went school shopping with Mom was the absolute worst part of the whole trip. All that off and on and rolling up of hems and adjusting of socks and underwear drove me up the wall. "Okay," I tell her instead. "I think it'll be fine."

"Hon?" Out of nowhere, a large woman with a blonde beehive appears. She has a mole on her chin and purple eyeglasses that are attached to a silver chain. My heart sinks. It's Mrs. Murphy, the owner of the store. "Oh, *Jack*!" she says. "I didn't recognize you, dear. You've gotten so tall!" She raises an eyebrow. "And your hair is so long!"

I have to force myself not to roll my eyes. Or turn and run in the opposite direction. Even Mom, who never said a bad thing about anyone, told Dad once that Mrs. Murphy was the biggest busybody she'd ever met in her life. "That woman could make a full-time career out of gossiping," she'd say, "and still have time left over to talk about something else."

"And this can*not* be our little Pippa," Mrs. Murphy coos. "My Lord, sweetheart, you're practically a lady!"

Pippa looks at her shoes. I'm not sure she remembers Mrs. Murphy.

"How're both of you *doing*?" Mrs. Murphy's voice is overloaded with concern now, probably because she hasn't seen us much since the funeral.

"We're fine." I take a few steps back, pulling Pippa along with me. The last thing I want to do is get into a conversation with Mrs. Murphy about Mom. Or Dad. Or anything having to do with our family. "We're just looking for some stuff for school. Thanks."

"You look awfully weighted down with all those clothes," Mrs. Murphy says, holding out her chubby arms. "Can I put them in a fitting room for you while you keep looking?"

"Oh no, she doesn't have to try anything on." I shift Pippa's clothes to my other arm, discreetly pushing her behind me. "I'm pretty sure we got the right sizes. We just have to get some shoes. And I have to get a couple of things, too. You know, jeans and stuff."

A look of concern crosses Mrs. Murphy's face as she glances around the store. "Is your father around?"

"No."

"No?" The eyebrow goes up again. "You're here all by your*self*?"

"I have a credit card, okay?" I don't mean to sound as rude as I do, but the look that flits over Mrs. Murphy's face indicates that I've already crossed that line. Next to me, Pippa reaches out and grabs one of the belt loops along the back of my shorts. I take a deep breath and reach into my back pocket. "I mean, my dad gave me his credit card. He said I could use it so that Pippa and I could get some school clothes, and that if there were any problems, you could call him at the car lot. Is that all right?"

"Oh." Mrs. Murphy blinks again, as if something has suddenly come into focus. "Well of *course* dear, that's just *fine*." She reaches out for Pippa's clothes again. "Why don't you let me hold these outfits behind the counter for you while you look for your things?"

I hand over the clothes, relieved that she's not annoyed with me. "Thanks," I say. "We're almost done."

"Jack, do you want any *help*?" Mrs. Murphy sounds slightly desperate for some reason.

"No, really. We're good." I hope I sound more polite. "But thanks for asking."

"All right then. The boys' section is on the other side of the store, and all the shoes are downstairs. Take your time. I'll be right over here when you're finished."

Pippa and I head downstairs where we each find a pair of sneakers and a pair of good boots. *Almost finished*, I think to myself as we traipse up the steps again and head over to the boys' department. Pippa is still as close to me as she can be without actually holding my hand, but I don't say anything. Ten more minutes, and we'll be done.

I head over toward a stack of neatly folded polo shirts near the back and grab four of them. Two navy, two hunter green. Perfect. Now I need a couple pairs of jeans, maybe a pair of khakis, and we're out of here.

"Y'all need any help?" A voice, soft as a flower, floats over the top of the polo shirts. I look up and feel my stomach do its second belly flop of the day.

It's the girl from the dock.

Chapter 9
PIPPA

Jack's eyes get all big and round when he sees the girl from the Andersons' dock. He takes a step back and bumps into a table covered with stacks of neatly folded sweaters. Two of the stacks tip over, spilling sweaters in lumpy heaps all over the floor.

"Oh my goodness!" The girl steps forward, giggling a little, and reaches for the sweaters. "Oh Lord, I just folded all of those!" She sounds amused for some reason, which surprises me. I'd be mad if I'd just folded a big pile of clothes and someone came in and knocked them over.

"Oh . . ." Jack crouches down a good distance away from the girl and starts grabbing sweaters. "Man, I'm so sorry."

"It's all right," the girl says, glancing over at him. "It actually happens more than you think. I keep tellin' Mrs. Murphy that we shouldn't pile these things so high, but she doesn't listen." Her voice has a distinct twang to it, something Southern maybe, like a cowboy. She's wearing a green T-shirt that says I HATE MAYO on the front, cut-off jean shorts, and pink cowboy boots with floppy little tassels on the side.

"Do . . . do you work here?" Jack's voice does this weird cracking thing, which has been happening a lot lately. It sounds like he sat on a tack right in the middle of a word.

"Yeah. Part time." The girl looks at Jack then, like really looks at him. Her pale eyebrows narrow suddenly. "Hey, were you layin' out on a really tall, flat rock this morning? Sort of around the corner from the Andersons' place?"

Jack stands up so fast it's like someone's jerked him up by his hair, and he steps right on my foot. A little grunt comes out of my mouth as I bend over. The girl gasps and looks right at me. "Are you all right?" She says "rat" instead of "right."

I nod, rubbing my shin.

"We have to go," Jack says, grabbing me around the wrist. "I mean, we have to go pay for our stuff. Sorry again about the sweaters. Nice to meet you. Bye."

He half drags, half pulls me to the cash register, leaving the girl behind to fold the rest of the sweaters by herself. *Not nice*, I think to myself. *Not nice at all, Jack*. Mrs. Murphy is behind the register, punching numbers into a little calculator and writing them down on a piece of paper. I have a hard time looking at her. Mostly because she talks a lot. A whole lot, almost like she's afraid of silence. And then there was the thing that happened at Poultney Pizza, where Dad took us one night for dinner a month after Mom died.

It was the first time we'd been outside the house, which was weird enough. Even though it was dark and warm, being outside again after so long felt like we were walking inside some kind of tunnel. Like the whole world had gotten smaller somehow, without us even noticing. I kept blinking when we walked inside the pizza place because the lights seemed so bright for some reason, as if someone had turned them way, way up. I spotted Mrs. Murphy right away as we walked over to the counter; she was talking a mile a minute to two other people at a table in the corner. As soon as she saw us though, she dropped her voice, leaned forward, and started whispering. I didn't hear anything, but I knew exactly what she was saying. Stuff about Mom dying of cancer. How sad it was that she'd left a husband and two kids behind. How none of us would ever be the same again, especially Dad, who considered Mom the love of his life. I knew this because I'd heard her say all of it to a bunch of other people at the potluck dinner we had after the funeral. And she had the same look on her face this time, too. Big eyes. Droopy mouth. Clucking lips. Not because she was actually sad for us. But because it was interesting. It was news. It filled the silence.

Now, Mrs. Murphy gives us a big smile. "Hello there,

you two! All set?" Her teeth are crayon-white. They don't look real.

Jack nods grimly. He stands with his back to the boys' department as Mrs. Murphy rings up the clothes. Every once in a while, he does this weird coughing thing in the back of his throat, like something's stuck in there, but I know nothing is. He's just nervous again, the way he's been getting lately whenever he's around girls. He turns into a total goofball when any of them get too close. And he goes completely bonkers when he actually has to talk to one. But I know that deep down, he's dying to talk to this one. Or at least find something out about her. So even though Mrs. Murphy is one of the last people on the entire planet I'd want to ask for something, I decide to help Jack out.

I take my notebook out of my back pocket. Jack looks sideways at me as I start writing, but he doesn't say anything. Finished, I put my pink glitter pen back in my pocket and slide the notebook across the counter.

Mrs. Murphy looks startled. "For me?" she asks, glancing at the paper. I nod. She leans in again, reading silently as Jack's face gets more and more puzzled. Then her face brightens. "Oh, you mean Shelby?" she beams, pointing to the girl. "Right over there?" I nod again. "Yoo-hoo, Shelby!" she calls, rolling up on her tiptoes. "Will you come over here for a minute, dear?"

Jack stares at me, furious. "Are you crazy?" he hisses under his breath. "What are you *doing*?"

I want to write, *"Trying to help you,"* in my notebook, but I don't have time, because Shelby is already standing next to Mrs. Murphy in her I HATE MAYO T-shirt and pink cowboy boots with the floppy tassels.

"Shelby," Mrs. Murphy says, putting an arm around her shoulder, "I want you to meet Jack and Pippa Kendall. They live on the lake, too, just a few houses down from where you're staying."

Shelby smiles. "Yeah, we sorta just met over there." She jerks her head in the direction of the sweaters, which, I notice quickly, have all been neatly refolded and stacked. "Y'all live on the lake?"

I nod.

Jack grunts.

Shelby smiles. She has a very pretty smile. "Cool."

"How old are you now, Jack?" Mrs. Murphy sounds very excited suddenly as she looks at him.

"Twelve," Jack mutters.

"Oh, and Shelby here just turned thirteen!" Mrs. Murphy puts an arm around Shelby and gives her shoulders a little squeeze. "And how about school, Jack? What grade will you be going into this year?"

"Seventh." Jack's eyes are boring a hole into the top of the glass counter.

"At the middle school, right?"

Jack nods.

"Oh!" Mrs. Murphy stares happily at Shelby's profile. "So will she!" She gives Shelby's shoulders another squeeze. "She's been so nervous about starting at a new school without knowing anyone, haven't you, dear? And now look! You've all met each other. Maybe you can even sit together on the bus!" Mrs. Murphy shakes her head. "I don't know about you, but I think it is absolutely for*tui*tous that you both came into the store today!"

Jack grunts and shoots me another dagger look.

But I'm not worried. He's embarrassed right now, but I'm pretty sure he'll thank me later.

And I don't know what the word *fortuitous* means, but the way Mrs. Murphy and Shelby are grinning, I'm pretty sure that's a good thing, too.

Chapter 10
JACK

I cannot bel*ieve* my little sister. Here I am, all choked up that she's communicating again after four months, and she goes and writes, "Who is that new girl over there?" in her freaking notebook! To stinkin' Mrs. Murphy, no less, who will probably get on some sort of secret intercom in her house and announce the whole story to the rest of the town by this afternoon.

I could kill Pippa. I really could.

Except that there's a little part of me that's actually kind of relieved. I mean, she did kind of just do me a favor, when you think about it. *I* wouldn't have said anything to Mrs. Murphy about Shelby, and I *definitely* wouldn't have talked to Shelby in school or anything. Not in a million years. I don't know why exactly, but girls make me nervous. Especially girls that look like Shelby. I'm always afraid I'm going to say something stupid or something that will make them roll their eyes. But now I'm actually a little bit ahead of the game, if you want to look at it that way. Now, thanks to Pippa, I know Shelby's name (which I never would have guessed, not in a million years), how old she is, and that she's starting seventh grade at Poultney Middle School next week.

Oh my God.

She's starting seventh grade at Poultney Middle School next week.

Which is the same grade I'm starting.

Which would be the coolest thing in the world if I hadn't just knocked over a whole table of sweaters she'd just folded and she hadn't seen me staring at her from Finster's Rock this morning.

I can feel my face burning just thinking about it. The sweater thing was an accident, but I don't know how I'll be able to explain the Finster's Rock situation. I'll have to lie if she asks me about it again. I can't come across as some kind of crazy person right from the start. She'll think I'm a stalker. A weirdo. My chances of getting to know her will be totally shot.

"Shelby's from Texas." Mrs. Murphy is still talking, but Shelby has leveled her big green eyes at me. Almost as if she already knows that I'm thinking about the rock. And lying about it. As if she's going to call me out on both.

I'm doomed.

"She's here just for the year, isn't that right, doll baby?" Mrs. Murphy asks. Shelby nods without taking her eyes off me. "The Andersons are Shelby's aunt and uncle," Mrs. Murphy continues. "And since I'm such good friends with Mrs. Anderson, we thought keeping our girl busy for a few days a week until school starts might be good for her just now." She rubs the side of Shelby's arm. "Help keep her mind off things."

Shelby drops her eyes when Mrs. Murphy says that. "It was nice to meet you both," she says, pulling out from under Mrs. Murphy's arm. "I'll see y'round."

Mrs. Murphy watches her walk back to her place in the boys' department and then leans over the counter. "You didn't hear this from me," she says confidentially, "but Shelby comes from a real troubled family. She's just here for a spell until things can get worked out at home. *If* they get worked out."

I don't know why this bit of information makes me angry. Maybe it's because it changes the way I've looked at Shelby up until that moment. That golden glow around her has just faded a little. Or maybe it's because the personal stuff about her wasn't Mrs. Murphy's information to give. She just took that away from Shelby, without even asking. Whatever it is, I just want to get out of this stupid store. Now.

"Can we finish checking out?" I ask, hurriedly adding, "Please?"

"Oh, of course!" Mrs. Murphy says, shaking her head. She starts tallying price tags again, tapping the numbers into the register. "Here I am, going on like a runaway train, while you two probably have a million other things to get to. I'm so sorry."

Between Pippa's six outfits, my shirts, and four pairs of shoes, the total comes to 236 dollars. It's a little bit more than I'd expected, but Dad said to get what we needed, and that's what we did. I still need to get some pants, but I'm not doing it today. No way, no how. I hand Mrs. Murphy the credit card and watch as she swipes it through the little black machine.

"It'll just take a moment," she says, smiling broadly.

I look away, stare down at the plastic earrings and shell necklaces beneath the glass counter. They look like little eyes glaring up at me. Accusing me of spying on Shelby.

"Hmmm . . ." Mrs. Murphy says, frowning. "This is saying the card's declined."

"Declined?"

"It just means something's off." She flutters her hand. "It's probably nothing. This is an old machine. It happens every once in a while. I'll try again."

I can feel myself start to sweat under my T-shirt.

Pippa tugs on my sleeve, but I don't look at her. "Hold on, Pip."

Mrs. Murphy's forehead furrows as she swipes the card again and taps on the side of the machine. I close my eyes. Beg silently for the machine to work. Hope that Shelby doesn't hear what's going on. Pray that what I think is about to happen doesn't happen.

I open my eyes.

"I'm sorry," Mrs. Murphy says. "There must be something wrong with the card, Jack. I've run it through three times now, and it keeps telling me it's declined. Does your dad have another one I can use?"

My heart plummets into my stomach. I take the card from her, shaking my head while simultaneously reaching for Pippa's arm. This is Dad's only credit card. And the only thing wrong with it has just hit me like a fist right between the eyes.

We have officially just moved from bad to worse.

Chapter 11
PIPPA

I'm scared. I haven't seen Jack this mad in a long time. He's even madder than he was inside Murphy's when I wrote the question about Shelby in my notebook. And he's hurting my wrist. I hang back when we get outside the store, twisting my hand until he lets go.

"Get on your bike," he says, already swinging a leg over his own. "And try to keep up." His voice is mean, which is scaring me even more. Jack hardly ever talks mean to me, unless something's really wrong.

It's hard to keep up. Jack's fast on his bike even when he's not mad. He swerves around people on the sidewalk, races through two stop signs without looking, and almost hits a lady walking her dog. "Hey!" she screams as he flies on past. "Where's the fire, buddy?"

I might have been more scared if I didn't know where he was going. But I know as soon as he turns into the alley next to the Poultney Flower Shop that he's headed toward the car lot on the other side of town. Mom always used to take us to visit Dad at work whenever we came into town, but it was Jack who showed me the shortcut.

Every few minutes, he checks on me, looking over his shoulder as he crosses a street or comes to the end of another block. But every time he does, he looks irritated, like he's mad at me for being so far behind. And even though there's so much distance between us, he doesn't slow down. Not once.

I don't understand what just happened. Mrs. Murphy told Jack that *declined* meant that something was off. Does that mean something fell off the card because it was broken? It didn't look broken to me. It looked perfectly flat. Maybe it was her machine, like she said, and she just didn't try enough times. Three doesn't sound like enough times to me. I think you should try at least five. Maybe I can write that in my notebook when we get to the car lot. Tell Jack to go back and let her try it a few more times.

Jack turns hard on Webby Road and starts pedaling to the top of it. Webby Road is a long, gigantic hill. At the top of it is Dad's car lot. I can already see the big red sign overhead: KENDALL'S AUTO SALES. I haven't been to Dad's work in a long time, not since Mom got sick, but the same proud feeling whenever I see our name up there rises in my chest. Dad started the car lot all by himself, when he was first married. Mom always said he was the best salesman in Vermont. I bet he's sold a thousand cars since I was born. Maybe even more than that.

I'm almost to the middle of the hill when I notice that Jack's gotten off his bike. But something's wrong. He's thrown it to the ground instead of leaning it on the kick-stand. And he's just standing there, staring at something. My heart starts to beat real fast as I keep pedaling. The steepest part is right before the top, and by the time I get there, I'm panting. Jack still hasn't moved from his spot. But he's put his hands on top of his head, and he's pulling at his hair.

I look over to where he's staring. Something seems weird, but I don't know what it is. I look more carefully. Dad's office, which is just a little white building off to the right, looks the same as always. There's the blue rocking chair Mom gave him for the front stoop and the gigantic stone flowerpot next to it. The blinds in the front window are closed, just the way I remember, and the American flag, which Dad hangs every morning, is flapping in the breeze.

"Where are the cars?" Jack whispers. His face is white. "Where are all the *cars*?"

That's when I realize what's wrong.

The parking lot next to Dad's office, which used to be filled with rows and rows of clean, shiny cars, is completely empty. Actually, that's not true. A blue Cadillac Eldorado is parked next to Dad's office. But that's Dad's car. The one he's been driving for the last ten years. Everything else is gone. Missing. Like some gigantic tornado came in and just swept everything away.

"There's nothing here." Jack starts walking toward Dad's office. "There's nothing left!" His voice is getting louder and angrier, and even though I'm scared, I run to catch up with him.

Because I don't know what's worse: being alone in an empty car lot, or staying with Jack to find out why.

Chapter 12
JACK

I knew something was wrong even before I got to the top of that stupid hill. I could just feel it. It was like the day Mom got the news about being sick. I was right outside the screen door to the kitchen, just about to come in, when I saw her hang up the phone and lean her forehead against the wall. She pressed her hands against it too, one on either side, like she was trying to hold herself up, and held still for a minute. I held still too, staring at a wrinkle on the back of her green-striped shirt, waiting. I knew something was wrong, but I never would have guessed in a million years that I would hear the word *cancer* when she told all of us about the phone call later that night.

And that's the same feeling I get when I crest the top of the hill and see Dad's car lot. Dad's *empty* car lot. I just stand there for a minute, staring at it like some kind of idiot. A weird sensation of dreaming comes over me, as if I'm in some long, airless vortex. The ground feels light beneath my feet, and my arms are tingling. Am I imagining this? Are there really *no more* cars in Dad's car lot? Does KENDALL'S AUTO SALES technically no longer exist?

My feet start moving with a mind of their own. And as they do, it's like the rest of my brain starts moving too. Where have the cars gone? Who took them? What has Dad been *doing* all this time?

I can hear Pippa behind me, trotting to keep up, and for a second, I think of turning around and telling her to go home. She doesn't need to hear any of this. She worries so much already; adding this to her pile will only make things worse. But I don't turn around. I don't tell her anything. Because another part of me wants her here with me. I know she's only ten and she doesn't even talk, but right now, having her next to me while I go find out the truth about this crazy situation might be the only thing that's keeping me from falling over.

Dad's sitting behind his desk when we walk in. He's talking on the phone and it sounds like he's trying to make a deal, but the way his face changes when he sees us tells me all I need to know. I'm so scared that I want to cry, which makes me so mad that I'm afraid I'll start screaming. And then, all of a sudden, just like that, I remember something.

It was Mom's last week in the hospital. Dad had taken Pippa down to the cafeteria to get her something to eat, and it was just Mom and me in her room. I was sitting on the ledge in front of her window, my feet propped up against the wall, watching her as she slept. She slept constantly that last week, but all the while she would moan and her lips would move, like she was having a bad dream. There were tubes everywhere, in her arms, below her nose, all attached to these stupid machines around her bed that beeped every few minutes. Her hair was gone then, but Dad had bought her a blue-and-purple silk scarf that the nurses tied over her head and fastened in the back so that the extra material draped over her shoulders like little ponytails. Blue and purple were her favorite colors, but I thought it looked terrible on her, like she was some kind of old person. And yet for some reason, despite the ugly scarf and the machines and the way her face would twist up while she slept, I thought she looked beautiful. I never took my eyes off her when I was there. Not once.

Which was probably why I almost fell off the ledge when I saw her eyes flit open suddenly and settle on me across the room. She smiled and patted the side of the bed next to her, and I went over and sat down as carefully as I could so that I didn't bump her or sit on any of the tubes. My heart was pounding out of my chest. I was scared that this was going to be it. You know, the end.

"How's my guy?" Her voice was just a whisper.

"I'm okay," I said, although it was the dumbest answer ever because first of all, it wasn't even remotely true, and second, I had no idea how I was anymore. Or how I might ever be again. I slid my hand under hers. "How do you feel?"

"Tired." She closed her eyes and then opened them again, searching my face for something. "I love you so much, Jackie. You know that, right?"

My nose was in full prickle mode, but it didn't matter. I could already feel the tears on my face as I nodded.

"You'll have to help Dad out as much as you can when I'm gone, okay?"

"I know, Mom."

Her fingers tightened the tiniest bit around mine. "It might be hard for a little while. But do whatever it takes. Promise me, honey." She paused, her index finger barely brushing mine. "Remember, Jack, family is everything."

It's the tiniest burst of memory, a flick of the wrist, but as it flashes through my brain again inside Dad's office, the anger that's been rushing through me seems to slow and then fade. *Family is everything. Promise me, honey.*

"Dad." My voice sounds hollow in my ears. "What's going on? Where are all the cars?"

"Terry," Dad says into the phone even as his eyes lock with mine. "I'll have to call you back, all right?" He puts the phone down slowly, inhaling through his nostrils.

"Where are all the cars?" I ask again, because it's the only thing I can think to ask, and he still hasn't answered me.

Dad stands up from behind his desk. Seeing him in his dress pants and shirt and tie makes me want to cry again, because I don't understand why he would get dressed for work if there's no work to go to. "They were repossessed," he says. "Taken away."

"When?"

He bites his lower lip. "About a month ago."

"A *month*?" That was right around when the blue vitamins showed up.

He doesn't answer.

"Why?"

He shrugs lightly. "That's what they do when a company goes out of business."

"So there's no Kendall's Auto Sales anymore?" I have to push the words out of my throat.

"No." Dad steps out from behind the desk and comes around to where we're standing. He takes Pippa's hand and puts his other hand on my shoulder. "I didn't want to tell you guys because I didn't want either of you to worry. But I'm on it, okay? Things are a little tough right now, but I've got a few things cooking on the back burner, and we'll be okay. I promise."

I look down at the rug. It's an ugly yellow-and-brown checkered pattern that Mom picked out when Dad first started. I don't know what she was thinking. It's hideous.

"Your credit card was declined," I hear myself say, even though I know it's probably the single worst thing I could say right now, like throwing gasoline on a fire.

But something in me doesn't care how big the fire might get or even how badly we all might get burned. I want answers. I *need* answers.

Dad looks startled for a moment, like someone's just pinched him. "The credit card I gave you last night?" he asks finally. "Are you sure?"

I nod. "Mrs. Murphy tried it three times, but it didn't work."

"So you didn't get any school clothes?" His face goes from shocked to angry in about three seconds. "Not one thing?"

"We couldn't." I shrug. "The card didn't work."

"Oh, and I bet Mrs. Murphy had a ball with that information, didn't she?" Dad starts pacing around the office, and since it is about the size of a shoebox, that means he only takes two steps, turns around, and then takes another two steps. "I give it until four o'clock this afternoon for everyone in Poultney *and* the lake to hear about this one."

"Who cares about Mrs. Murphy?" I say, hoping he'll calm down. Even if he is right. Next to me, Pippa slips her hand into mine.

"Nobody cares about Mrs. Murphy!" Dad's face is getting red. "She just makes it her business to care about everyone else!" And just like that, the fire moves from a flicker to a whoosh of flame.

"Dad, listen . . ." I'm trying to remember what Mom used to say when he'd get mad like this around her, but nothing comes. Maybe it's because he never got mad like

75

this around her. They were always laughing. He always had his arms around her, his nose in her hair. My brain feels like a vacuum, like it's just a tornado of whooshing hot air in there.

"No, you listen." He stops all of a sudden, mid stride, and whirls around. "You go back right now and tell Mrs. Murphy . . ." He breaks off for a moment, thinking. "Actually, you know what?" He opens one of his desk drawers, pulls out a phone book and rips it open. Then he starts punching numbers into the keypad of his phone. His nostrils are white around the edges, and his eyes look wild. The fire is crackling, threatening to spread.

"Dad," I say, taking a step forward. "It's okay. It really is."

"Oh, I know it's okay," he answers, and his voice trembles a little around the edges. "I'll make sure— Hello, Mrs. Murphy? This is Sam Kendall calling. I understand my chil—" He pauses, listening for a moment. Something pulses in his jaw, and he rubs a hand over his face, as if scrubbing it clean. "Yes, they told me all that. I'm not sure what the problem is just yet, but I'd like to ask you to keep the clothes they picked out so that I can come in later and settle the bill. Yes. Yes, that's right. Thanks very much. Yes, I appreciate that. Yes, Mrs. Murphy. Yes, absolutely. Thank you. All right. Good-bye."

He hangs up the phone, flicking his eyes up to meet mine. And in that moment, I see something that I've never seen before. He looks frightened. More than frightened, actually. Terrified. Which makes me more scared than I've ever been in my life. Even more than when I knew Mom was dying. As terrible as it was, there was an end to things when Mom died, a closing of a door. Dad is standing just inside his door. And there's no telling if he's going to keep it open—or slam it right in my face.

"Dad?"

He blinks twice and just like that, the frightened look vanishes.

"Don't you worry," he says, coming around the desk and putting his arms around the both of us. "I'll find a way to figure all this out." His hand tightens on my shoulder. "I promise."

Chapter 13
PIPPA

I don't let go when Dad drops his arms. I know something's wrong, and it scares me. I love him so much. And I know that he will take care of everything, just like he said. He'll find a way to make it okay again. I know he will. He always does. He promised.

But Jack just stands there looking at him with a strange expression on his face. "How're you going to figure all this out?" he asks. "You don't have a job. We don't have money." There's a weird tone to his voice. It's not shaky. It doesn't crack. It almost sounds like he's daring Dad to answer.

I squeeze my arms around Dad even more tightly. *Don't get mad*, I want to say. *Jack doesn't mean to give you a hard time. He's just scared. He loves you. He does.*

But I can feel Dad tense under me. "I will *find* money," he says firmly. "And I'm not going to talk about this in front of your sister. Both of you need to go home now and let me take care of things."

Jack opens his mouth as if to say something else, but Dad beats him to the punch. "Jack, please. You're just going to have to trust me."

Jack closes his mouth.

"Go home." Dad leans down and kisses the top of my head. "See if Nibs needs any help in the garden. Maybe Mr. Thurber will be back." I look up and smile at him. His eyes look sad. Worried.

"I'll see you later, baby," he says, tweaking my nose. "Everything will be all right."

―――――――――

But everything is not all right with Jack. Usually when we're on Route 30, he rides right next to me, making sure that he's on the outside, closest to traffic, but now he rides way up ahead, like I'm not even there. I watch and wait, but he doesn't turn around or check over his shoulder. He just keeps moving ahead, getting farther and farther away.

I pedal faster, but when I do, my bike chain starts making a loud clicking noise. I don't know anything about bike chains, but every time I hear the sputtering noise, I slow back down again. *Please turn around. Please, Jack. Slow down and look at me.*

It's getting hard to breathe. The sun is directly over-head, beating on the pavement. Route 30 is nothing like Lake Road. There are no trees for miles. Just long, endless fields of grass on both sides of the long, hilly pavement.

79

Plus, there's not a cloud in sight. It must be ninety degrees at least. I wish I'd worn my Red Sox baseball hat. I wish I was a boy so I could take off my T-shirt and wrap it around my head. I wish Jack would turn around. I wish . . .

I wish.

I can hear a car coming up behind me. My fingers tighten around the handlebars as I guide the bike off the side of the road and onto the soft, gravelly edge. Up ahead, Jack disappears around a bend. *No! Don't leave me!* The car is getting closer. I clench the handlebars until my knuckles turn white, trying to keep the bike steady. One awkward lurch and I'll fall right into the ditch next to me. Tips of long grass brush against my calves. A mosquito flits against my neck and then buzzes along the edge of my ear. I reach up to swat it away.

Whoosh!

The car flies by. My bike teeters and then wobbles like a windup toy. The handlebars go right and then left and then somewhere in the middle. Somehow, I stay upright and the bike doesn't fall over, but tears roll down my cheeks as I steer the bike out of the gravelly edge and back onto the road. They keep coming as Route 30 turns into the quiet shade of Lake Road and then, as I realize Jack is nowhere in sight, they stop.

I don't care if he's upset with Dad. And I don't care if he never talks to me again. He has no right to just leave me like this. Mom must've told him a hundred times that he has to always keep me in his sight whenever we go out on the road together. Always. When I get home, I'm going to walk right up to him and punch him in the shoulder. Hard.

I pedal furiously, cruising down Lake Road as fast as I can. Tall pine trees on both sides of the road fly by in a blur, and the breeze snaps like a sheet against my face. Suddenly, the bike sputters one last time. The gears lock with a quick lurch, and then they stop altogether.

I'm in the air for about three seconds before I hit the ground. A sharp pain shoots through my right knee, and I grab for it with both hands. My bike is behind me, the front of it twisted at a weird angle. Next to it is the chain, lying in the dirt like a black snake. I sit for a minute, panting. Stunned. My knee feels like it's been ripped off. I lift my hands slowly off the top of it and look. A quarter-sized flap of skin has been peeled all the way off in the middle. The skin around it looks burned. Scaly patches of pink, rubbed raw. Blood trickles from all of them. I bite my lower lip and rock back and forth. Little sounds come out of my mouth—*unh, unh, unh*—without me even trying. It's at least another mile to the house. How am I going to get this dumb bike back there all by myself?

"Pippa?"

I jump at the sound of my name and whirl around. Shelby steps out from behind a pine tree on the other side of the road. Her green T-shirt has been knotted in the front, and she's pulled her hair up into a ponytail.

"Are you all right?" she asks in her funny accent. "I saw you fly off your bike back there, and I came runnin'. Are you hurt?"

I nod, glancing down again at my knee. Her cowboy boots make a crunching sound as she walks over and the tassels sway like little bells. She squats down next to me. "Can I see?" Her ponytail hangs down between us as she leans in close. She smells like suntan lotion and sunflower seeds. "Ugh," she says, grimacing. "You ripped the skin clean off. That'll leave a scar, probably. But a good one. A story scar." I must look confused when she says that, because she rolls up the sleeve of her T-shirt and points to a mark on her arm. It's lighter than the rest of her skin and shaped like a kidney bean.

"This is a story scar," she says. "I got it from a dog who knocked me to the ground when I was real little and tried to bite my arm off. The only reason he didn't is because a nun who was on her way to church came runnin' across the street and wrestled him off me."

My eyes widen. A nun? Wrestling a dog?

"See?" Shelby grins. "It's a good story, isn't it? And because of the scar, I'll never forget it. Now you have one, too." She nods. "A scar and a story."

Some story, I think to myself. My dumb brother leaves me behind on our way home and I wreck my glittery bike. How exciting.

Shelby looks down the road. "I'm pretty sure I saw your brother go sailin' past 'bout ten minutes ago. He didn't feel like waitin' around for you, huh?"

I shake my head.

"I guess brothers can be like that." She gets back up and walks over to my bike. "Although, I wouldn't know. I don't have any." I want to ask her if she has any sisters, and I want to ask her what she was doing in the woods, and if she really does hate mayonnaise like it says on her shirt, but of course I can't. She bends over and picks the chain up out of the dirt. "Lordy, no wonder you went flyin' off this thing. Your chain here fell clear off!"

I smile a little, mostly because she talks funny and also because Jack will kick himself from here to China when he finds out about all this later. Serves him right. And he won't be getting any more help from me when it comes to finding out information about Shelby. I'm done being nice to him.

She examines the chain in her hands, peering at the links up close. "You mind if I fiddle with this for a minute?"

I shake my head as she gets down on her knees and holds the chain up alongside the bike. "I think your chain's too long," she says finally. "Okay with you if I take out some of the links and then put it back on?"

I nod, watching her nimble fingers move along the chain and snap off three of the links. She grunts a little as she reattaches the remaining links and then tugs the whole thing once, like pulling a rubber band, to test it.

"All right," Shelby says, moving over to the bike. "Let's get this thing back on and get you home so you can fix up that knee."

A tiny river of blood has snaked its way down to the middle of my leg. It's already started to dry, the edges crinkling a little like dried paper.

But it doesn't hurt as much as it did before.

In fact, I think to myself as Shelby settles me on the handlebars and gets on the seat behind me, *it hardly hurts at all*.

Chapter 14
JACK

I'll go back for Pippa. I will.

But right now, if I don't pedal as hard as I can, until the muscles in the front of my legs start to shake and burn, until the noise inside my head settles down, I will explode.

You're just going to have to trust me, Jack. Dad's words hammer in my ears as my wheels race along Route 30. Trust him? After he's been getting up every morning and putting on a shirt and tie and leaving to go to a job that doesn't exist? No wonder the electricity has been turned off. No wonder his credit card didn't work. There's no money left! What if Pippa and I hadn't shown up today? How much longer would he have gone on pretending that he was selling cars? And what exactly has he been *doing* instead? My eyes burn, thinking of him sitting behind his old brown desk, staring into space, drawing little circles on his desk calendar.

Although he *was* on the phone today. So maybe he's been making some calls. But to whom? Who *do* you call when your wife dies and your business flops and you run out of money? If you're Dad, the answer is no one. Not Grandma and Grandpa Kendall out in Wyoming, not Mom's big brother Uncle Leon, who lives in Florida, not even Reverend Jim from church, who came and sat with us at the house for two whole days after the funeral, until Dad finally told him to go home. Even after we first found out that Mom was sick, Dad didn't want anyone's help. "I can handle it," he told Grandma Hession, who came out anyway and stayed until Mom finally told her to go home.

And he did handle it, I guess. He hung a big calendar chart on the front of the fridge that listed all of Mom's doctor's appointments and chemotherapy sessions. After those stopped working and Mom had to go into the hospital, he made sure he got there every single day to spend time with her. All while still working at the car lot and getting Pippa and me up for school every day and making sure we ate dinner and showered and did our homework. It was like he had extra arms or something and just carried everything for as long as he could. And then, when Mom died, he kind of let go, I guess. Maybe his arms just got too tired, holding everything up for so long all by himself. Maybe he just had to sit down again and take a breath.

I pedal harder, grateful for the ache in my legs, the

shortness of breath in my chest. It keeps the tears at bay. I will be the person he can turn to while he takes a break. I'll do whatever it takes. I don't care. I can get a job mowing lawns or washing dishes at Perry's Restaurant in town. I'll even get down on my hands and knees and scrub the floor every night with a toothbrush if I have to. Just until we get back on our feet. Until Dad has rounded the bend again. *We can do it*, I think to myself, braking so hard in our driveway that the bike nearly falls over. I stand there for a minute, panting.

We can.

———————————————

Three-quarters of the way back down Lake Road, I stop my bike and stare. Someone is riding Pippa's bike. And it's not Pippa, because she's sitting in the middle of the handlebars, clutching both of them for dear life. The only thing I can see of the other person is a pair of pink cowboy boots.

My stomach nose-dives.

I get back on my bike and race toward them.

"Pippa!" I shout, waving an arm over my head. She deliberately turns her head in the other direction. Behind her, Shelby's head appears. She puts a hand on Pippa's back and brakes as I pull up next to them.

"What happened?" I wince, looking at Pippa's knee. It's all busted up. There's blood everywhere.

"Her chain fell off," Shelby says coolly. "I fixed it, and now we're pedalin' back."

"Her . . . you . . . I mean . . . How . . ." Not one of the questions in my head can be formed into a coherent sentence.

"Listen, she's hurtin'," Shelby says, sidestepping my shocked expression. "We need to get her home so she can get this knee fixed up and bandaged."

"Yeah, of course," I say quickly. "Here, why don't you ride my bike and I'll take her the rest of the way? I mean, you're probably tired, right?"

"Actually, I'm fine." She says "fan" instead of "fine." "We're almost there anyway." She leans forward. "You okay with that, Pippa?"

Pippa nods, still avoiding my eyes.

"Okay," I say. "Let's go, then."

I fall in next to Shelby, pedaling as slowly as she does as we move along the rest of Lake Road. I look at the trees on the other side so that she can't see my flushed cheeks or the way I keep biting my lip. Now I'm not only a stalker, but I'm also a total jerk, leaving my little sister behind like that, and not being around to help when she got hurt. I sneak a peek at Pippa, who's staring down at her knee like I'm not even there. I know she's steamed. And she has a right to be. Leaving her on Route 30 was a stupid move. A selfish one, too. I didn't even look back at her, to check like I usually do. Not once. Mom would be so disappointed.

"Pippa," I say.

She's busy with her knee, pressing the scraped side of it with the tip of her finger.

"Pippa." I make my voice louder. "Don't touch it yet, okay? We need to clean it first, get all the germs out."

She stops and looks in the other direction. It's a deliberate move. Another door closing.

I move my bike in closer, so that I'm slightly ahead of Shelby, and lower my voice. "Listen, Pip. I'm sorry. I really am. You have every right to be mad at me, but I promise I won't do that again. Ever. Okay?"

She doesn't turn her head. Doesn't even blink.

Shelby does, though. She speeds up a little, flicking a glance in my direction, and then shrugs, like she's making an excuse for Pippa's silence.

"Thanks for helping her."

"Sure." She sidles a glance at me.

"I thought you were at work," I hear myself say. "At Murphy's?"

Shelby nods. "I'm just there 'til noon, and only on Mondays and Fridays. Mrs. Murphy was goin' to take me home, but I told her I'd walk the rest of the way when we got to Lake Road. That's how I saw Pippa."

I don't know what to say to that, so I don't say anything.

"You're the little blue house up there, right?" Shelby asks.

"Yeah."

"It's cute. I like the cat shutters."

"My dad made those for my mom," I say without thinking. "She used to love cats."

"She doesn't anymore?"

I look ahead, wishing I could stuff the last sentence back into my mouth. "She died. In April."

It's the first time I've said the words *Mom* and *died* out loud. To someone other than myself. I don't like the sound or the feel of them. They have sharp, jagged edges and they drag along the soft parts of my mouth.

"Oh." Shelby bites the side of her thumb. "I'm sorry."

"Yeah." My nose prickles, thinking of all the people who said those exact same words at the funeral. *I'm sorry. How awful. I'm sorry. How sad. I'm sorry. I'm sorry. I'm sorry.*

Besides being annoying, it was confusing, too. Why were *they* sorry? They didn't have anything to be sorry about, and neither did I. Losing my mother was not a sorry kind of thing. It was bigger than sorry. Much, much bigger.

"So y'all live with your dad, then?" Shelby asks.

"Yeah." What a strange question. Who else would we live with?

"I think I saw him last night while I was out on the dock. Gettin' out of a blue car?" She slides another glance at me. Her eyes are pale green, like celery.

"Yup, that's him."

"He looks nice." She sounds wistful.

"He is nice." Up ahead, I can see the lilac bushes in our front yard, the corner of our yellow mailbox behind them. How did we get here so fast?

Shelby stops pedaling when we reach our driveway and puts her feet on the ground. "Home sweet home, Pippa."

"C'mere, Pip." I swing a leg off my bike and kick out the stand. Then I reach for her, putting my arms around her back so that I can carry her inside. But she pulls away from me and kicks at me with her good leg. "Pippa!" I stand back, rubbing the arm she nailed. "Come on! I'm just trying to help you get off the bike!"

She stares at me deliberately and then hops off by herself, wincing as her bad leg comes in contact with the ground.

Shelby smiles, watching her hobble toward the house. "She's a tough lil' cookie, huh?"

I nod.

"I think she was really scared, bein' alone like that. 'Specially after she fell and all."

I stare at the ground.

The front door slams.

"She doesn't really . . . talk?" Shelby asks.

"No. Not since . . . everything happened with my mom."

Shelby nods, as if understanding this perfectly. "Well, good for her. People talk too much anyway." She raises her hand and starts back down the driveway. "See y'all later."

And just like that, she's gone.

Chapter 15
PIPPA

The bathroom is upstairs, which means I have to hop up the steps using my good leg. It takes forever. I can only do one step at a time, because every time I move, my ripped-up knee throbs. I jump up another step and wince as the ball of pain behind it pounds and pulses.

I want Mom.

My hands are holding the railing so tight that my wrists hurt. Another jump. And then a third. By now, my knee hurts so badly that I wonder if there is a tiny, separate heart on the inside of it, beating with pain. I put my head down on the railing.

I want Mom. I want Mom. I want her arms around me, and her soft voice in my ear telling me everything is going to be all right, that all we have to do is put a warm washcloth over the torn-up skin and rub a little ointment on it and I'll be good as new again.

I clench the banister and hop up another step. And this time, as fire shoots through my kneecap, I realize that nothing will ever be as good as new. Not ever again. The thought of this forces a sound I've never heard before out from the back of my throat. It sounds like a goat bleating and a baby crying, and even though it scares me, I hang on to the railing and let it go.

"Pippa!" Jack bursts into the house, staring up at me. He looks frightened, like he did at the car lot, but the sound in my chest just keeps coming and coming, like water from a tipped-over jar. Jack bolts up the steps and grabs me, sliding one arm around my back and the other underneath my legs. "It's okay, Pippa," he says, barreling up the rest of the steps and kicking open the bathroom door. "It's okay. It's okay. I'm here."

This time I don't kick him. I don't flail my arms or try to punch him or hit him on the shoulder.

I just wrap my arms around his neck and hold on.

———————

"You're still worried about Mr. Thurber, aren't you?" Nibs grunts as she yanks a particularly stubborn weed out of her garden and straightens up. A big smear of dirt sits just at the top of her forehead, like a thick, lopsided rainbow, and the knees of her overalls are dark with mud.

It's twilight. The sky stretching across the lake is a periwinkle blue, the sun just a lemon slip of memory. Kind of like the day we just had. Almost over. Almost gone.

Nibs turns her head, looking out across the water, and sighs. "You've got to have faith, Pip. He'll come back before he leaves for the winter. I know he will. Herons love to check on things before they take off. They're very conscientious animals." She reaches down for another weed. "How's the knee? You feel all right?"

I nod, glancing down at the white bandages. It hurts, but not nearly as much as before. No more throbbing or pulsing inside. It's just sore, mostly.

"Your brother did a nice job cleaning you up," Nibs says. "He's a good boy, Jack."

He did do a nice job, although it took him over twenty minutes to wipe the dried blood off my leg and clean all the dirt and pebbles out of the wound. I held on to his neck with both arms as he poured liquid from a brown bottle over the whole thing. It fizzed and sizzled and stung like five thousand bees, but he kept talking real softly to me and telling me that it would be over soon, and when he squirted on some ointment and wrapped gauze around it and fastened it with tape, it really did start to feel better again. Afterward, he made me a peanut butter sandwich and sat with me until I fell asleep on the couch. When I woke up, he wasn't there anymore. But Nibs was outside, working in her garden, so I went out to sit with her.

"Where'd he go, by the way?" Nibs straightens up again and scans our property with a gloved hand. "I haven't seen hide nor hair of him for the last few hours. He all right?"

I'm not one hundred percent sure, but I point to the tree on the other side of our yard.

"Tree house?" Nibs asks.

I nod. It's where Jack always goes when he needs to think.

Nibs squints into the distance. "Well, what's he doing, sleeping up there? He's not working on that floor again, that's for sure. I haven't heard any hammering." She pauses, winking at me. "Or any swear words."

I smile a little and nod. Jack doesn't actually say a lot of bad words, but when he does, we usually hear them drifting down from the tree house.

The sound of a car on the road behind us makes me turn around. I gasp a little and sit up straight. It's the blue Eldorado.

Dad! I limp toward it as fast as I can, patting on the window with my hand before it comes to a stop. Dad's eyebrows narrow as he turns off the engine and gets out of the front seat. The tie he was wearing earlier is gone, and his dress shirt is unbuttoned, the sleeves rolled up to his elbows.

"What happened to your knee, sweetheart?" He bends down and examines the bandage, touching the edges of it gently. "Did you fall off your bike?" I nod. "But it wasn't too bad, was it? This bandage looks good and tight. Did Jack help you out?"

I nod again and put my arms around him. He's home! Early!

Dad glances over at Nibs and then kisses the top

of my head. "Listen honey, I have to talk to Nibs for a moment. Would it be too much trouble to run inside and make me a few peanut butter sandwiches? You can just throw them in a bag. I'll take them with me."

I pull away. He's not home early. He's just home to do something quick and then leave again. My eyes fill with tears. "Oh honey, if it's too much . . ." Dad starts, but I shake my head, fiddle with the hem of my shorts. A tear slides down my cheek. He squats down so that he's at eye level with me and wipes the tear away with the pad of his thumb. "I'm sorry I have to leave again, Pip," he says softly. "But it's just because I'm trying to make things better for us. It won't always be like this. I promise. It's just for right now. Just for a short time. Please try to understand. Don't be angry."

I put my arms around his neck and hug him tightly. If only I could tell him that I'm not angry, that I've never been angry. I just miss him. I want him home the way he used to come home, right before dinner when he'd swoop me up at the door and put me on his shoulders. He'd dance around the house, holding both of my hands over his head like a giant puppet, and then he'd make his way into the kitchen, where Mom was making beef stew or chicken pot pie, and pull her away from the stove and spin her around the floor. My stomach would fill with butterflies, looking down from my perch at the tops of their heads, and when they pressed their foreheads together, I would slide my hands around the backs of each of their necks, feeling as if my heart would burst. I'd give anything for that again, just once.

I'm halfway to the kitchen when I see Jack looking out the window of the tree house. I wave with both arms and point to Dad. Jack's face darkens and then disappears. My stomach tightens. He'd better not come down and start an argument. Dad's trying so hard.

I make a few peanut butter sandwiches, wrapping them neatly with tinfoil and settling them inside a paper bag. I add two cans of orange soda and a bunch of paper towels so Dad can wipe his hands, and then I take out my pink glitter pen and write DAD in big pink letters on the front. Underneath his name, I draw a heart and a smiley face. Finished, I glance back out the kitchen window. Dad is still talking to Nibs, who's wiping her hands on the front of her overalls and nodding. Jack's there too, just standing quietly. No sign of any arguing. I grab the bag of sandwiches and hobble out the door.

"Hey, sweetie." Dad takes the bag from me and peeks inside. "Thank you so much. You make the best peanut butter sandwiches, you know that?" He puts an arm around my shoulders and squats down so that I can see his eyes. "Listen, I have to go do some business in Middlebury tonight, and I have to take Jack with me. We won't be back 'til late. Nibs said she'd stay with you." He squeezes my arm. "You okay with that?"

I glance over at Nibs, who gives me a wink.

I pull out my pink pad from my back pocket and write: "Why can't I come?"

Dad stares at the little pad for a moment and then looks back up at me. "Where did you get that?"

I point to Nibs.

He glances up at Nibs, his face flushing. "Wow," he says after a moment. "What a great idea. Thank you."

Nibs smiles.

I tug on Dad's pants and point to the pad again. I want to know why Jack gets to go with him and I don't.

But he shakes his head. "It's something only Jack and I can do right now. I'll explain it to you later, okay?"

I scowl and write again on the pad. "What time will you be back?"

"I'm not sure," Dad says. "But late, honey. You'll be asleep."

I slide my pen and pad back in my pocket. I feel a little heartbroken, but I don't know how to write that down on my pad. And after that, there's really nothing left to say.

Dad leans over and kisses me on the cheek. "I'll bring you back something, all right? A surprise." He gives my nose a tweak. "Be good for Nibs. Remember your manners." He stands up straight. "Get in the car, Jack. I just have to grab a few last-minute things inside."

I stand in the middle of Lake Road and wave after Dad and Jack leave. I wave and wave until the blue

Eldorado becomes a little dot on the road and then disappears around the bend. I know that I just have to get through tonight and then go to sleep and that when I wake up I will see them again, but right now, it feels like a really long time.

"It's supposed to be a nice night," Nibs says, returning to her weeding. "Maybe we'll build a little fire in the pit and make s'mores after dinner. Would you like that?"

I nod and stare out at the lake.

Sometimes, if I look hard enough, I actually think that I can see Mr. Thurber. A funny-shaped tree branch will look like his beak, or the outline of a cloud will really, for a split second, look just like one of his wings. But then I'll blink or rub my eyes, and I'll know it wasn't real. That I just imagined it.

I trace the outside of my bandage with the edge of my thumb. I'm glad it's there. If it wasn't, I might wonder if I imagined getting hurt, too.

Chapter 16
JACK

It's kind of amazing how fast things can happen sometimes. How you can be flat on your back in a tree house
one minute, trying to figure out what to do, and in a car
with your dad twenty minutes later, driving toward the
Great Unknown. I'm going to call it that for now, because
I don't have any idea where we're going or what's going
to happen when we get there. All I know is that Dad
wants me with him, which, if you consider all the stuff
he's been keeping from me in the last few months, feels
like a pretty big deal.

"I can't believe I didn't think of getting Pippa a little
notepad like that," he says as we get to the end of Lake
Road. "I must really be out to lunch."

Lunch and dinner and maybe breakfast, too. "It's
okay," I say out loud. "I didn't think of it either."

"It's such a simple thing." He shakes his head as he
pulls the car onto Route 30. "God Almighty."

He sounds so sad just then that I reach out and put a hand on his shoulder. "You've had a lot on your mind, Dad. It's okay." He might've missed the boat when it came to finding a way to help Pippa communicate, but at least he's not the one responsible for her not communicating at all. And for just this second, I'm glad he's not. If there was one more thing on his shoulders, he might collapse.

"I'm glad she has Nibs," Dad says. "I really am. She needs someone like that around."

Someone like that. I guess he means an adult. A woman. Someone who can be a friend and maybe even a little bit like a mother at the same time. Not Mom, of course, but someone a little bit like her.

"She's had her own share of heartache," Dad goes on. "Nibs, I mean. I think she kind of gets it."

"What do you mean? What kind of heartache?"

"Mom never told you?"

"Told me what?"

Dad puts on his blinker and settles in behind a bright red Honda Accord. "She lost her husband and her little boy in a car accident. A long, long time ago. Down in South Carolina, where she used to live."

Something in my stomach twists. A hollow sound rings in my ears. Hearing something like this—out of the blue—about someone I've known all my life feels as if the floor has just dropped out beneath my feet. "I . . . I didn't even know she was married."

"Happily married." Dad accelerates past the red

Honda. "At least that's what Mom said. They talked about it a few times, I guess."

Why didn't Mom ever say anything? Maybe it was too private. Too hard to talk about.

"So . . . I mean, what happened?" I ask. "There was a car accident?"

"Nibs was driving through some pretty bad weather." Dad's voice is grim. "Rain, sleet. The baby was in the back in a car seat, and her husband was up front, sleeping. A tractor trailer coming the other way started sliding and just barreled into them. She didn't know what happened until she woke up in the hospital two days later." His jaw clenches. "She was the only one who survived."

I press my lips together, stare numbly at the passing scenery.

"Sometimes I think people go through certain things so that they can help the rest of us make sense of the stuff we don't understand." The trees outside the window are coming back into focus. The fields are fields again. The sky the same sky. "You know, the hard stuff. Like with Mom. Or maybe that's just true of Nibs. You know what I mean?"

I think I know what he means. Maybe a little bit.

Or maybe I don't.

"They'll have fun tonight." Dad's shoulders relax a little as he pulls off an exit that reads MIDDLEBURY. "I don't think there's any rain in the forecast. Maybe Nibs'll build a fire."

I sit up as the highway sign disappears behind us. "Wait," I say. "We're going to Middlebury?" Middlebury is over an hour away. And except for the time Mom took Pippa and me there once so we could get a real Ben & Jerry's ice-cream cone, we've never spent any time there. There's no reason to. Middlebury is a rich town with big, fancy houses and expensive storefronts. Not really our kind of place.

"We are indeed." Dad's fingers clench around the steering wheel.

"You know someone there?"

"Not exactly."

"Then why are we going?"

"We have a job to do. In town."

"We do?" I feel excited suddenly. "Oh Dad, that's great. I was just trying to think of ways that I could help out, you know? Like with the bills and stuff. I was even going to go down to Perry's and ask . . ."

"Oh no." Dad cuts me off with a wave of his hand. "Absolutely not, Jack. One, you are twelve years old. It's not even legal for you to work yet. And two, I don't ever want you going into town and giving people the impression that we're so bad off that you have to wash dishes or scrub someone's floor. You hear me?"

His voice has escalated so steadily that by the time he finishes talking, I've pressed myself all the way back into the seat. "What are you yelling for?" I ask.

"I'm not yelling. I'm just telling you how things are going to be."

"Fine." I cross my arms over my chest. "Whatever."

The car rolls on in silence for a few moments. How is it that we've just had one of the longest and most substantial conversations since forever, and in the next second we're arguing? What's wrong with him? What's wrong with me?

"I'm sorry, buddy." Dad puts his hand on mine. "I know you're just trying to help. I really do. And I appreciate it more than you know."

I stare straight ahead, forcing myself not to shrug his hand off mine. It sure doesn't sound like he appreciates it.

"Jack, look at me."

I hate it when he does this, taking his eyes off the road for a few seconds so that he can make eye contact with whomever he's talking to. I used to watch him from the backseat when he'd do it with Mom, my heart leaping around like a jumping bean until he'd finished what he had to say and shifted his attention back to driving. Now, I give him a quick glance and then look away again. "You're supposed to keep your eyes on the road."

"Fine." He turns his head again. "But I need to tell you something and I want to make sure that you hear it."

"I'm sitting right next to you."

"I'm not talking about hearing with your ears. I'm talking about hearing it here." Dad taps his chest with two fingers. "Inside. Where you can keep it."

I don't say anything. Part of me still wants to give him a hard time for snapping at me, but another part of me wants to tell him that I've heard every single thing he's ever told me in my entire life and that it's all in there, that it will always be in there, forever and always. "Okay," I say softly.

He takes a deep breath, puffing his cheeks with air, and lets it out again. "You know how much I loved your mother, right? How much I still love her. How much I'll always love her."

"Yeah." My nose starts to tingle.

"And you know how much the house meant to her. I mean, it was her whole world."

"I know."

The lake house had always been Mom's baby, passed down through several generations. I knew Grandma and Grandpa Hession had given it to her as a wedding gift and that it was her pride and joy. She even referred to it sometimes as her "mini Taj Mahal," telling friends that it was just as beautiful as any palace in India. She'd grown up in that house, fishing off the dock, blowing out her birthday candles on the kitchen table, and learning how to drive up and down Lake Road. She'd even met Dad there, after he'd been accidentally invited to her high school graduation party and walked into the kitchen to ask for a can of orange soda. It had always been Mom's house. Her heart.

"She left it to me when she died," Dad says. "So it's mine now. And when the time comes, it'll be yours and Pippa's, which means that maybe one day you'll be able to give it to one of your children."

I nod, staring out the window. *Where is this conversation going? And why do my armpits feel sweaty all of a sudden?*

Dad takes another deep breath. "Do you know what a mortgage is, Jack?"

"Like the money you give to the bank every month to pay off the house?"

"Exactly. And a few years ago, even though Mom owned the house, she and I took out another mortgage so that we could fix it up some more. You know, add in that bathroom upstairs and build on the deck."

"So you're still paying that mortgage back?"

"I am." Dad reaches up and yanks on an earlobe. "Or at least I should be. Here's the story, buddy. I'm really, really far behind on the mortgage. Which means that the car lot isn't the only thing that's going to be a distant memory if I don't do this job in Middlebury."

"Okay." I sit up a little straighter. "Well, whatever it is, Dad, let's just do it."

He nods, biting his lip. "It's just—" He clears his throat. "I want you to know that it . . . well, it's not a good job."

It feels very still in the car suddenly, as if all the molecules and particles in the air have come to a stop. "What do you mean?"

"It's . . ." he starts again. "It's a bad job, actually."

My brain is racing. What is he saying, exactly? And what *isn't* he saying? "Bad, how?"

"Against the law," he says again. He turns his head and looks directly at me. "But here's the thing, Jack. We won't get in trouble. We won't get caught. And once it's over, I'll be out of the woods. I'll be able to make the mortgage payments I've missed, get the electricity turned back on, buy you and Pip some good school clothes. We'll be able to get a little bit ahead so that I can go out and find real work. Good work. I just . . ." He looks back at the road. "I can't lose that house, Jack. I just can't. After taking care of you guys, it was the only thing your mother asked of me before she died. I can't lose it, do you understand? I've got to do whatever it takes to make sure I don't lose that, too."

Of course I understand. I understand perfectly.

Do whatever it takes. Promise me, honey.

I understand more than perfectly. It actually makes complete, logical sense.

So why have I never been more terrified in my life?

Chapter 17
PIPPA

I hold out my arms as Nibs piles things into them: a large plastic bag filled with green pepper chunks, tomato slices, and jalapeño peppers; another plastic bag filled with Italian dressing and strips of raw chicken; two whole lemons; and a large bundle of wooden skewers.

"All right," she says, wiping her hands on the front of her apron. "Take that out and put everything on the table next to the pit. I'll be right behind you in a minute or two."

But I don't move. Nibs didn't say anything earlier about vegetables or raw chicken. And she certainly didn't mention anything having to do with lemons. I hate lemons. They make my eyes water and the inside of my mouth pucker.

"You can wipe that pout right off that pretty face of yours," Nibs says, already bustling around the kitchen again. "I know you're waiting for the s'mores ingredients, but I'm not pulling any of them out until you have a decent dinner. Meats before sweets, my mother always said, and she was absolutely right. Besides," she continues, nodding at my knee, "your body is in recovery mode. Do you expect it to do all its fixing and healing if you're only running on sugar?"

I give her a look. But I already know I can't argue with her. I hadn't thought about my body needing good stuff in it so that my knee will heal. I hate it when adults are right. It's so annoying.

"We'll have them after dinner," Nibs says, giving me a pat on the butt. "Don't you worry. Now get on out there."

Nibs' fire pit is much smaller than ours, but it's prettier to look at. Pizza-sized stones have been arranged neatly around the edge like seats, each one painted a different color. My favorite is the light red one, which is not quite pink but close enough, and it is just wide enough for me to sit on with my legs crossed. Nibs has already gotten a small fire going; it crackles and sputters, shooting tiny red sparks high in the air.

I set the bags of vegetables and chicken down on the little picnic table and look out on the lake. The sky is a pale lavender color, but it won't be dark for another two or three hours. The only movement on the water is a red motorboat pulling a lady on skis. She's wearing a green bathing suit and a bright orange life jacket. A sheet of dark hair flies out behind her as she skims over the surface of the water. I watch for a moment, marveling at how easy it looks from here. I know very well, of course, that getting up on those things and then balancing your-self behind a boat that's moving thirty miles an hour without falling over is a whole other story.

Dad used to water-ski all the time, although I can't remember the last time I saw him out there. He and Mom didn't have enough money for a boat of their own, but they would rent one every summer, and Dad would be up behind it every chance he got. He was good, but my favor-ite part was being on the boat with Mom. She drove those boats so fast that sometimes I was afraid I'd fly out, my arms and legs cartwheeling in the air like one of those cartoon characters you see on TV. My hair would slap my face like tentacles, and I would lose my breath when-ever she made a sharp turn. But it was magic, flying and floating like that, all at the same time. Like being sus-pended over the top of a gigantic plate of water, just under a blue bowl of sky.

The lady behind the red motorboat disappears around the bend in the lake. The water in her wake rocks and shifts and then quiets again. Somewhere in the distance, a bird shrieks. My stomach tenses, but I know it's not Mr. Thurber. He only makes noises in the morning, and they sound like a frog snoring. Or the faint pitter-patter of stones flung into the lake. Nothing like a shriek. Nothing like a bird at all, come to think of it.

I turn to go back inside when another movement catches my eye. Shelby is sitting on the Andersons' dock, just like she was this morning, with her legs dangling over the side. This time though, her legs are bare, and she's chewing something and then spitting it into the water. I creep over to the large pine tree that separates Nibs' house from the Andersons' and peek out.

Thwoot! Shelby spits again, this one higher and farther than the first. I'm impressed. I've never been able to spit very far, but I sure would like to. I move to one side, trying to get a better view of her, and step on a twig. It makes a sharp cracking sound. Shelby turns her head at the noise and waves in my direction. I duck back behind the tree.

"Pippa?" she yells. "Is that you?"

I don't move. My cheeks are hot. I feel stupid that she caught me spying. Especially after everything she did for me today. Maybe if I walk straight back, she won't see me. If I can get over to Nibs' house again, I'll just—

"Pippa?"

I jump as Shelby appears, striding toward me across the Andersons' lawn, and clap my hand over my mouth. She laughs, showing small, white teeth, and fingers a small bag of sunflower seeds. Her orange flip-flops practically glow in the fading light. "What'cha doin' behind a tree, silly?"

"Hi, Shelby!" Nibs says, coming out of the house. "We're cooking out tonight. Would you like to join us?"

I look at Nibs and then back over at Shelby. They know each other?

"That's real nice of you," Shelby says. "But I don't want to intrude. If you and Pippa are—"

"Don't be silly!" Nibs waves her off with one hand. "We'd love to have you, wouldn't we Pippa?"

I nod.

"All right!" Shelby grins. "Thanks. Let me just tell Aunt Leslie."

Nibs frowns as she looks at me and puts a hand on her hip. "Now what did you just get all over yourself?"

I look down at the smear of dried sap across the front of my shirt. It must have rubbed off when I was leaning against the tree, spying on Shelby. "Go change right quick," Nibs says, pointing to the house. "We still have a few minutes before dinner. And bring me that shirt. You'll never get that sap off if you don't soak it first."

I head into the house. It's cool and dark inside. No lights, I remember. No electricity. But a blob of red in the middle of the living room floor catches my attention. Is it one of Jack's shirts? A pair of Dad's shorts? I walk over, thinking what slobs they both are, how many times Mom used to tell them when she . . .

But it's not one of Jack's shirts.

I bend over and pick it up. Hold the silky material in my hands, studying the black pattern along the front.

It's not a pair of Dad's shorts, either.

I don't know how long I stand there, staring at the Spider-Man mask in my hand. I have the weirdest feeling then, like a bell ringing somewhere in my head, but it's so far back I can hardly hear it.

I slip my fingers through the eyeholes and wiggle them around. It must be Jack's. He used to have all the superhero suits when he was younger, from the Hulk to Aquaman, before Mom packed them away in the attic. But why would it be out here? He doesn't play with them anymore. The last time he even mentioned superheroes was, like, five years ago. Way before Mom got sick. And even back then, the one he really used to be obsessed with was Superman. He was always kind of lukewarm about Spider-Man.

"Pippa! You change your mind about dinner?" I jump a little as Nibs' voice sails through the window. "Come on, sweets! Chicken's almost ready!"

I toss the mask on the couch and head upstairs to get a clean T-shirt.

Dumb boys and their superhero costumes.

They don't know anything.

Chapter 18
JACK

"We're not going to kill anyone, are we?" I try to laugh after the question, but my mouth is as dry as sand. I need water. I need air. I need a paper bag, in case I have to puke.

The car swerves sharply to one side. "*Kill* anyone?" Dad repeats. "No, Jack. Of course not. What kind of person do you think I am?" He reaches out and grabs the top of my arm until I turn and look at him. "No," he says again. "No, no, no."

"Okay. Well you said it was bad. I just didn't know how bad."

"It's not murder-bad, for Pete's sake." Dad drops his hand from my arm. Beads of sweat have formed a small ridge along his upper lip. "I'd never *hurt* someone."

"Then what is it?"

He doesn't answer right away. For a moment, I'm not sure he's heard me. His gaze, locked on something in the horizon beyond the windshield, is so intense that, for a split second, it reminds me of the way Mom's eyes looked on that last day in the hospital. She'd taken one last gasp and then stopped breathing altogether, and even though I knew she wouldn't start back up again, that this was really it, I felt the tiniest bit relieved that the terrible rattling sound that had been coming out of her chest every time she inhaled had finally stopped. The thing I didn't expect was the way her blue eyes sort of froze into place right afterward, wide and unblinking. It made her look frightening. Like someone else. Someone I didn't know.

Suddenly, Dad blinks.

"We're going to take money," he says slowly. "Out of a bank."

"But I thought you said you didn't have any money," I say stupidly.

"I don't," Dad says. "That's why we're going to take it."

A long, silent moment passes. Something inside my chest lurches. "You mean without asking?"

Dad nods.

"You're going to *rob* a bank? That's what you're saying?"

"That's what I'm saying."

I reach for the dashboard. Press my fingertips against it. Try to laugh, which doesn't work. Again. "Yeah, right."

"I'm serious, Jack."

"No, you're not."

"I've never been more serious about anything in my life."

Another long moment passes. The taillights of the car in front of us look very red for some reason. Almost as if they're not real.

"I don't have any other choice, Jack. I'm completely out of money. I can't get a loan because my credit stinks. And I—"

"Tell Grandma and Grandpa!" I burst out. "I know you hate talking to them, but just tell them. They'll help you. You know they will."

"I already did." He shifts in his seat. "Right after I lost the car lot. It just about killed me, but I called them up and explained the situation. They sent me some money and I . . . I went and invested it in those stupid vitamins because the guy promised me I'd triple my money in a month's time." He winces, as if someone has just pinched him. "You know how that turned out. So I can't call them again. I won't."

"There's got to be someone else then," I try. "Someone you—"

"There isn't. Jack, I'll lose your mother's house if I don't get this money, and I won't be able to live with myself if that happens. I know it's wrong. Believe me, I do. It's completely, one hundred percent wrong."

"Then don't do it! Dad, you could go to jail!"

"I'm not going to go to jail. I wouldn't be doing this if I didn't absolutely know that I wouldn't get caught."

"How can you say that? Of course you can get caught! They have guards and stuff. Inside. With guns!"

"Not the bank we're going to."

"How do you know?"

"Because I checked."

"Dad." *Oh my God. This can't be happening. He's not actually saying this to me. I'm not actually in this car, sitting next to him, because this is just some crazy, warped dream, and it's not really happening.*

Right?

"Jack. I know. Believe me, I know. Nothing you can say to me right now isn't something that I haven't already said to myself. But I've got to protect my family. I'm only doing this for my family."

My nose is tingling. Bad. Like on both sides and all the way up and down. For a second, I don't even care if I start crying; I really don't. Maybe it will stop him. Maybe if I throw a fit, it will . . .

Do whatever it takes, Jack. Promise me.

I look out the window. A brown-and-white cow is standing in the middle of an enormous pasture, chewing grass. *Dumb cow,* I think to myself. *Dumb, stupid, lucky cow.*

"We have an hour before the bank closes," Dad says. "So we'll go in and just look around for a few minutes. Get our bearings."

"Right now? To*day*?"

"As soon as we get there."

"Dad, I can't."

"You don't have to do anything, Jack. Just look around. Get the lay of the land. See how things are set up, where the tellers are sitting, where the exit is."

The tellers? The *exit*? I feel dizzy. My stomach is churning.

Whatever it takes, Jack. Please. Family is everything.

But not something like this, right? Mom would have never agreed to something like this!

Dad's voice drifts in from somewhere in the distance. "I'll do everything. It's a very small bank. There are only two tellers: a man and a lady. All you have to do is distract the guy so I can do my business with the lady."

"What do you mean distract them?"

"Make a scene or something. So he's not paying attention to me."

"What kind of scene?"

"Well, let's talk about it. What would you feel comfortable with?"

"NOTHING!" My voice cracks, shooting up an octave. "I wouldn't feel comfortable with anything, because this is completely crazy! You sound like a lunatic! I can't even believe you're considering this, let alone asking me to—"

My voice, which has been at a near scream, starts to fade as Dad pulls off the highway and slows the car. He puts it in park, pushes the hazard lights on, and turns so that he's facing me. "Jack."

"NO!" I kick the underside of the dashboard. Once. And then again. "No, no, no, no, *no!*" Each word is followed by another kick, until Dad reaches out suddenly and grabs me.

"All right!" he says. "Enough!"

His hands are gripping the tops of my arms so hard that I can't move. I always forget how strong he is. And then I look at his face. It's all crumpled up, and for a second, he looks like he might cry. Like really cry, the way I saw him do at the potluck dinner after the funeral, when he walked outside by himself and stood on the front porch. The house was still full of people, and Mrs. Murphy was yammering away in the middle of them and it had gotten too hot, almost unbearably hot, no matter what room I was in, and so I started to follow him. But I stopped when I saw him lean against one of the porch posts, his hands shoved deep inside his pockets, his head low against his chest. Without warning, his shoulders started to shake, very lightly at first, as if he had sneezed, and then gaining strength, until he covered his face with his hands and sank down heavily against the porch railing. His whole body trembled and heaved and I wanted to go to him, I did, but something told me not to. Something held me in my place.

But Dad doesn't cry in the car. He lowers his head instead. Breathes in hard through his nose. Raises his face again. "I don't have any other choice right now, buddy." His voice is calm and steady. "I've got nothing left in the bank." He lets go of one of my arms and forms the letter "O" with his fingers. "Zero. You know how the electricity got turned off yesterday? Well, the same thing is going to happen to the water. The bank has given me two more weeks to get some money together before they take the house altogether, and I just can't let that happen. Okay? I won't let it happen, Jack. Not to us. Not to your mother."

Behind him, the headlights from passing cars swell, illuminate the car, and then fade again. Every time one of the lights passes over Dad's face, I see something different in it. Something I've never seen before right there, in his eyes. It frightens me. So much that even though I want to start kicking again, I sit still. I sit very, very still and don't move, not even when he lets me go, turns the hazard lights back off, and pulls the car back onto the highway.

We're silent the whole rest of the way, which is only about ten more minutes, until he pulls off at the Middlebury exit and turns into a wide parking lot. To the right is a brick building with tall windows and white shutters. Pink rhododendron bushes line the sidewalk in front, and a wrought-iron lamppost stands still as a guard. Hanging from the lamppost is a wooden sign, with the words MIDDLEBURY BANK in neat black print. Panic fills me again, like a flash of heat.

"Dad, please. Don't do this."

He shuts off the car. Turns to look at me. "I already told you, buddy. I don't have any other—"

I lurch as his eyes flick up, glancing at something over my shoulder, and whirl around. A guy is coming out the front door of the bank with an envelope in his hand. He doesn't look too much older than Dad, but he walks with a limp, his right foot trailing a little behind him. For a single, crazy second, I think about running out of the car and asking him to help me. But what would I say? My dad's lost everything, including his mind, and he's about to go inside and rob this bank? He'd probably laugh in my face. Tell me to go take a hike.

"That's the guy I told you about," Dad says, watching in the rearview mirror as the man takes a left and limps down the sidewalk. "Which means just the lady should be in there. I'm going in." I turn back around as Dad checks his watch. "We've only got about thirty-five more minutes until they close."

I cross my arms over my chest, stare straight ahead. "I'm not going." It's my last card. Hopefully, if I refuse, he'll change his mind. He wouldn't do it alone, would he?

Dad hesitates, scratching behind his ear.

I hold my breath. *Pleasepleasepleasepleaseplease.*

Then he reaches into the backseat and pulls out a pillowcase. "You shouldn't go," he says, riffling through the pillowcase. "It was wrong of me to ask you. I'll be fine."

My heart plummets into my stomach as he keeps rummaging around inside the pillowcase. "What's that?" I ask as I find my voice again.

"Just a few things I—" His forehead creases. "Damn it."

"What?"

Dad closes his eyes. "Nothing. I just . . . I had a—you know, something to cover my face. I must've dropped it when I was rushing around the house, grabbing my stuff."

What stuff? I want to ask him but I can't. I'm too scared.

Dad gets out of the car and opens the trunk. I can hear him tossing things around—*Plish! Plam! Plunk!*—and then the heavy, final thud of the trunk slamming shut again. He opens his side of the car and slides back in, holding some kind of silky blue thing.

"Dad, please." I can feel a sob in my throat.

He shoves the blue thing into his pocket and reaches inside the car, gripping the sides of my face with both hands. "You get in the backseat of the car and stay there until I come out." His fingers tighten around the back of my head. "I never should've asked you to come, buddy. I'm sorry. Stay here. I'll take care of everything, okay? I promise. Just sit tight."

And before I can blink, he's slammed the car door and disappeared.

Chapter 19
PIPPA

During dinner, I find out three things about Shelby that I didn't know before:

1. She's allergic to eggs and shellfish.

2. She met Nibs the first day she got here, after an exploding oven sidelined Shelby's aunt and uncle, who were supposed to pick her up at the airport, and Nibs offered to go instead.

3. Her mother and father (who she calls Momma and Pops) are getting a divorce.

The eggs, shellfish, and exploding oven topics don't seem to bother her much. But when the subject of Momma and Pops comes up, Shelby stops chewing and drops her eyes. Her smile fades as she mumbles something I can't hear.

"What was that?" Nibs asks.

Shelby tugs at her earlobe. "I said that's why I'm here," she says to her plate. "You know, in Vermont. Instead of Texas."

Now Nibs stops chewing. "Because of the divorce?"
Shelby nods.

Nibs sidles a glance at me, and I wonder if she wants to ask Shelby what her parents' divorce has to do with her being here, too. Maybe they all needed space? Or maybe Shelby just wanted to get away for a little while?

But Nibs doesn't ask any more questions. Instead, she stands up, and with the tip of her shoe, shoves a log farther into the fire. "Sometimes it's good to get away from home," she says. "Being in a new place can help you see things differently. Give you a new perspective on just about anything." Red sparks fly up like miniature fireflies, and a sizzling sound drifts out from underneath the logs. It's almost dark, except for a few pale clouds on the horizon, which sit like empty benches in the sky. The crickets have started to chirp, and somewhere in the distance an owl hoots.

Nibs looks up from the fire. "Who's ready for s'mores?" she asks, reaching for our plates. I nod and grin as Shelby claps her hands. Nibs laughs. "You two stay here. I'll be right back."

Shelby's sitting on a blue rock three over from mine. She looks over at me as Nibs goes inside and twirls a strand of hair around her finger. "So what grade are you going into?"

I hold up four fingers.

"Fourth?"

I nod.

"That means you're how old?"

I hold up ten fingers.

She raises her eyebrows. "You're only ten?"

I nod.

"Wow. You must be smart. I didn't start fourth grade until I was eleven." She rolls her eyes. "Momma held me back in first grade. I didn't take too well to the teacher."

I stare at her flip-flops, wondering what "didn't take too well to the teacher" means and where her pink boots are. I wish I could ask her if I could try them on. See what they feel like. I've never worn shoes with heels.

Shelby squints at me, as if trying to see something up close. "You ever talk out loud?"

I shake my head.

"To anyone?" she presses. "Ever?"

In response, I reach around and pull out my notebook.

"Ohhhh, you write stuff down?"

I nod.

"Is that what you're goin' to do in school?"

I nod.

"Your teachers okay with that?"

I shrug. I don't know if they'll be okay with it. This has never happened before.

"Well." Shelby looks into the fire. "I guess they'll have to be, won't they? It's not like they can force you to talk." Her face tightens in the light of the flames. Shadows flicker across her neck and arms like camouflage.

"Graham crackers, chocolate bars, and marshmallows, anyone?" Nibs bangs open the screen door and reappears with her arms full. For the next hour, as darkness settles over us like a blanket, we toast our marshmallows on sticks, stuff ourselves with s'mores, and stare up at the stars. Nibs lights her pipe and points out the Big Dipper, and tells Shelby about Mr. Thurber and how Mom saved him as a little baby heron back before we were even born, but after that it's mostly quiet. For a long time, the only sounds are the crackle of the fire and the soft lapping of water against the shore. I can feel my eyelids starting to get heavy when suddenly, out of nowhere, Nibs says, "You know, I moved up here from the South too. Long time ago."

My eyes fly open. I remember Mom telling us once that Nibs was originally from South Carolina, but that was all she ever said about it.

"Why'd you move?" Shelby asks.

Nibs opens and closes her lips around the stem of her pipe. It reminds me of a fish, gasping for breath. Even in the shadows, I can see her eyes change, like a shade being drawn. "I needed to go somewhere and start fresh," she says slowly. "Get a new perspective on things, like I said before."

I arrange my arms behind my head so that I'm more comfortable. This is the first time I've ever heard Nibs talk about anything personal. Actually, except for the fact that she's a teacher and likes to garden, I don't really know anything about her personal life at all.

"And did you?" Shelby asks.

Nibs wrinkles her nose. "Did I what?"

"Get a new perspective on things," Shelby says.

Nibs pulls again on her pipe. Tiny puffs of smoke drift from the corners of her mouth, and the clean, spicy scent mingles among the firewood. "It's been thirty years," she says finally. Her voice is soft. "I guess if it hasn't changed by now, it never will."

Shelby nibbles on a nail. "So is that a yes or a no?"

Nibs smiles. She stands up and winces as something in her knee cracks and pops. "Maybe it's a little bit of both." She turns her pipe over, tapping the bottom of it gently so that the contents spill into the fire. "Well, ladies, it's time to turn in." She points at me. "I promised your father I'd have you in bed by nine." She looks at her watch. "It's a quarter of. We have fifteen minutes to keep me an honest woman."

"Good night," Shelby says, waving. "And thanks. I really appreciate you askin' me."

"We'll do it again," Nibs says. "Sleep well."

It's darker inside our house than it is outside. "Lord," Nibs says, feeling along the wall for a light switch, "you should try to at least keep one light on when you leave the house, Pippa. Especially at night. It's like a tomb in here."

I hold my breath as the sound of her clicking the switch echoes throughout the room. "This light doesn't work?" she asks finally. I shake my head. "How about the kitchen?" She steps carefully around the furniture, holding her arms out in front of her, and then flips on the kitchen switch. Nothing.

"Pippa?" Her voice floats through the dark house. "Sweets, why don't any the lights work in the house?"

I shrug.

"You've probably got a blown fuse." Nibs opens a cupboard and takes out a glass. "That pipe always dries my throat out. Let me get myself a nice glass of water and then I'll go downstairs and check the fuse box."

I stand in the doorway, watching her make her way over to the kitchen sink. A half moon shines through the window just above it, illuminating the faucets and the silver basin. Nibs turns the handle on the right, but nothing comes out. She frowns and tries the other one. Nothing.

She turns around, staring at me through the watery darkness. "Pippa," she says. "The water's not working either." I look down at my shoes. I didn't know the water wasn't working, but I feel guilty for some reason, like I've done something bad.

"Honey," she says, coming toward me. "You've got no electricity and no water. What's going on?"

Chapter 20
JACK

I already have one leg over the front seat of the car as Dad gets out, and I drop down into the back of the car as he shuts the door. *BAM!* I jump at the noise and press my hands over my ears. Squeeze my eyes shut. Will not hearing or seeing anything in the next ten minutes mean it won't happen? That it isn't real? I arrange myself inside the narrow space between the seat and the floor and curl up into a ball. Is Dad inside yet? What will he say when he goes in? How long will it take?

"Mom." Her name comes out of my mouth in a sob. In all these months, I've never once talked to her out loud. Why would I? She's not here. Reverend Jim told us at the funeral that she was with God, waiting for us in heaven, but I'm pretty sure heaven is just some made-up place that people tell you is there to try to make sense out of everything and keep things all nice and pretty. Sort of like Santa Claus or the Tooth Fairy. Stupid, dumb stories that people created to try to explain things they don't have the slightest idea about. The only thing I know for sure about Mom is that she's not here with us anymore, which means there's a good possibility I'm just talking to the wind. Still, right now, it's all I've got.

"Mom. You've got to help me. Please. He's doing this for you and I don't know how to make him stop. Please help me. Please show me what to do."

I wait, holding my breath. The air inside the car is stifling, the seat upholstery itchy against my face. He wouldn't pull out a gun, would he? He doesn't even a have a gun! Mom was the one who taught me how to take a hook out of a fish's mouth, because he couldn't stand to look at them that way, flopping around on the dock with a piece of metal stuck inside their cheek. Maybe he has a fake gun. Something that looks just real enough so they can't tell the difference.

"Mom." My voice cracks. *"Please."*

I don't know what I'm waiting for exactly, or what I hope might happen, but nothing comes. No brilliant idea, no comforting message, not even a feeling—an inkling—that she's heard me.

Instead, Ben pops into my head. I think about how much I miss him. And how mad I was when he said that we were still the only big news in town. I think about the way his face looked when I called him a big, fat idiot, and how I told myself I didn't care, because at that minute I wanted to hurt him the way he'd hurt me. But what I didn't realize until just this moment is that hurting Ben yesterday was a hurt on top of a whole other line of hurts—ignoring him all these months, not calling him back, even brushing him off at the funeral, when he tried to shake my hand outside of the church. I didn't mean to do that, either; it just happened. Calling him an idiot yesterday was the last straw. Even I know that. Which means that when we start school on Wednesday, I'm going to be totally on my own. For the first time since second grade. No Mom. No Ben. No nothing. I've got nothing left.

Suddenly, I'm pushing my way out of the car and racing across the parking lot toward the Middlebury Bank.

The front door is slightly ajar, which means that I don't make any kind of noise going inside. There is a tiny foyer just inside the door, almost like the one in the funeral parlor, all done up in rich red carpeting. A globe-sized lamp with gold spindles coming out on all sides hangs from the ceiling, and a full-length mirror has been arranged on the wall behind it. I catch a reflection of myself— wrinkled blue T-shirt, khaki shorts, chin-length, raggedy brown hair—and for a split second, my breath catches in the back of my throat. Is that really me? Am I really here?

Then I hear Dad's voice. "Yes, ma'am. That's right."

It's coming from the room directly to my right. My heart is throbbing in my ears, but I take a step back slowly, trying to angle myself behind the wall that leads into the room while trying to see into it at the same time. All I can make out is the floor, which looks like white marble of some kind, and three large windows with white drapes along the far wall.

"You can read it again, if you need to." Dad's voice drifts out of the room again. It's muffled, but it sounds firm and relaxed at the same time, as if he's at Lowe's talking to a salesman about lawnmowers or potting soil.

I sidle a little to the right. Before I faint, I just need to make sure . . .

His back is to me, but I can see some kind of blue mask pulled over his head, fastened with bits of Velcro. Tufts of hair stick out from the bottom of it like strange fingers. A lady with blonde hair and red lipstick is stuffing stacks of bills into the pillowcase. She does not look scared. On the contrary, her lips are pursed tight, and she's squinting her eyes at Dad. She moves slowly, deliberately, as if she has all the time in the world.

"Hurry up," Dad says. "I don't have all day. Let's go."

The lady clenches her jaw and tosses the money into the bag a little faster. The cubicle next to her is empty. That must be where the man with the limp sits. I glance behind me suddenly, looking for him. What if he just went to get a coffee somewhere? What if he walks through that front door again in the next two seconds? What will Dad do then? What will I do?

"Come on." Dad takes a step toward the lady. "Move it!"

The woman pauses, giving Dad another dirty look. "You won't get away with this," she says coolly. In her hand is a stack of bills wrapped with a blue cuff.

"I didn't ask you to say anything," Dad says tersely. "Just keep going."

The lady bites her lower lip, shoves the money with the blue cuff in the bag, and pushes it across the counter. "That's everything."

Dad grabs the pillowcase and raises his left hand. My stomach flip-flops when I realize there's no gun, and every muscle inside my body freezes. "Thank you for your time," he says. "You have a good day, now."

He keeps walking backward, just staring at the lady. She keeps glaring at Dad, as if daring him to try anything else.

Dad walks backward until he reaches the foyer. Then he nearly falls over me as he lurches for the door. That's when I see the mask up close. It's my Batman one, from upstairs in the attic.

"Jesus," he hisses, grabbing my arm. "You practically gave me a heart attack. Let's go!"

He holds on to me as we race down the steps, past the rhododendron bushes and the neat sidewalks, across the wide, smooth driveway, letting go only when we reach the car. It's at that moment, two seconds before we get into the vehicle, when I'm the most terrified, sure that the guy who works there will reappear suddenly on the sidewalk, or the woman will come bursting out of the building, or a police car will come screaming into the driveway.

But nothing happens.

It's as quiet as the lake in the morning.

Still as a funeral parlor.

And when Dad shoves me into the front seat and tosses the pillowcase on the floor next to me, I realize that another moment has gone by and still nothing has happened. He rips the Batman mask off his face and gets into the front seat. The car roars to life, and he backs up so fast that I fall forward, catching myself with both hands against the seat, and then tip back once more as he presses down on the accelerator. We shoot out onto the street and fly down the length of it, pausing only to make a sharp right-hand turn.

It takes us five minutes to get back on the highway and for Dad to settle the car in between a tractor trailer and a green Jeep Cherokee. He's going at least ninety miles an hour, but he tells me to take my seat belt off and crawl into the back and watch for cop cars. I do what he says, plastering myself against the back windshield, frantically looking, but I don't see any cops. Not a single one.

Ten minutes later, we reach the exit that will lead us back home.

The traffic is thinning out by now. The light is fading from the sky. In the distance, the green mountains loom like giant shoulders. Somehow, my heart is beating more slowly. My breathing is back to normal.

Still no cops. In fact, hardly any traffic at all, except for an old, rusted pickup with an enormous woman behind the wheel, and a blue Mercedes driven by an old man in a straw hat. The woman, who keeps looking at something down in her lap, barely notices as we fly by, but the old man peers out his window at me. I shrink down, sure that he knows, positive he's a plainclothes policeman.

After thirty more minutes, Dad pulls off at an exit called Weston. He glances at me in the mirror as he drives the car down a narrow, poorly lit road for a while, then steers it into a Friendly's parking lot.

"What're you doing?" I ask, glancing at the restaurant out the window.

"I'm starving," he says, catching my eye. "How about a decent meal before we head home?"

I stare at him dumbly. "You . . . you want to eat?"

He nods. His eyes still have a little bit of that wild look to them, as if some part of him is missing. As if something has been torn out. "You're not hungry?"

No, I'm not hungry. In fact, I don't know if I'll ever be hungry again.

"Didn't . . . ." I stare at the floor, as if searching for the words down there. "Didn't Pippa make sandwiches?"

"I want a real meal," Dad says. "No offense to Pippa, of course. I haven't had a decent, sit-down dinner in months. And neither have you. Let's go in there and get ourselves some meatloaf and mashed potatoes with gravy and big ice cream sundaes for dessert. What do you say?"

The thought of meatloaf makes me queasy. And yet the idea of being able to sit down in front of a plate that doesn't have a peanut butter sandwich or a hot dog on it doesn't seem so terrible all of a sudden. "What if there's someone in there?"

"Like who?" Dad leans forward and examines his face in the mirror. I wonder if his eyes look any different to him.

"I don't know. Anyone. A cop. Or just someone who recognizes us."

"We'll be fine." Dad opens the car door. "We can sit in the back if that makes you feel any better. Come on."

I watch as he gets out of the car and heads toward the front door of the restaurant. He stands there for a moment, holding it open, waiting for me. But I don't move. Not yet. I realize suddenly that if I decide to get out of the car just now and follow him inside, I will never be able to undo that decision. There's no turning back. It's like jumping off a cliff and deciding halfway down you've changed your mind. Impossible. What if going in there with him is the wrong decision? And what if this one wrong decision leads to a whole other set of wrong decisions? What then?

"Hey, buddy?" Dad lifts his chin, looking at me. "You coming, or what?"

But maybe it's not the wrong decision. Maybe it's just going inside a Friendly's restaurant, sliding into a red leather booth, and eating a meatloaf dinner with my dad.

"*Jack?*" Dad's voice is louder. He holds a hand out, palm up, a "what's going on?" gesture.

I take a deep, deep breath.

And then I slide out of the car and follow him inside.

SEPTEMBER

Chapter 21
PIPPA

"Stop pulling on your shirt," Jack says at the bus stop. "You're going to stretch it before you even get a chance to wear it."

I turn around, but not before sticking out my tongue at him. I don't know what he's so irritated about. Or why he's been all worked up for the past few days. He came up behind me on Wednesday and ripped the newspaper right out of my hand. Right while I was reading it! I tried to get it back, but he just pushed me away and walked outside. He thinks because he's older than me, he can do whatever he wants. Well, it's getting annoying. It really is.

I give the bottom of my new shirt another tug, just to let him know he's not the boss of me, and hitch my new backpack along my shoulders. The backpacks were extra, something that Dad surprised us with after coming home two days ago with all the clothes that Jack and I picked out at Murphy's. Packed inside were tons of new notebooks, packages of pens and pencils, calculators, and even a mini whiteboard with magnets on the back and a matching pen for my cubby.

"Good, right?" Dad beamed as I threw my arms around him afterward. "Did I do okay?"

I nodded and glanced over at Jack, who was sitting on the couch, scowling. Again.

"Jack?" Dad asked. "You got everything you need in there? Anything I missed?"

"Nope." He stood up, slinging the backpack over his shoulder, and walked out of the room.

I watched Dad watch him go. Dad's jaw was tight, and his eyes were sad, which made my stomach twist around inside. I put my arms around his neck and held him close. *You kept your promise,* I wanted to say. *Just like you said you would. You made everything better. It's okay.*

Now, Jack's face brightens a little as Shelby appears at the bus stop. She looks nice, dressed in a soft white skirt that comes to her knees, a short-sleeved denim shirt, and her pink boots. But except for the bag of sunflower seeds that she's holding in one hand, she doesn't have a single notebook or pencil anywhere on her. For a moment, I wonder if she's going to school at all. Maybe she's just here to wave us off.

"Hey y'all." Her boots crunch against the gravel, and her hair, which she's pulled up high into a ponytail, looks like it's been curled at the tips. "Day one of jail time, right?"

Jack smiles, but just a little. "Depends on who you get for homeroom."

"Oh, I doubt it." Shelby rolls her eyes and inserts a few seeds into her mouth. "They're all the same."

Jack scuffs the toe of his new sneakers against the ground. "Where's your books and stuff?"

"Don't have any yet."

"When are you going to get them?"

"Don't know," Shelby says mysteriously. "I kinda like to take things as they come."

Jack gives her a look that says he doesn't understand her answer either.

Shelby looks over at me. "You see Mr. Thurber anywhere yet?" I shake my head no, pushing down a knot of annoyance. Ever since she came over to Nibs' place for dinner, Shelby's made it a point to ask me about Mr. Thurber every chance she gets. I know she's just trying to be nice, but it feels weird too, like she already thinks she knows him or something. The truth is, Mom was the only person who really knew Mr. Thurber. Which means that he knew her too. Which also means that if something in his heron brain understands that she's never coming back, maybe he won't, either.

No. I don't want to think about it. I won't.

"Nibs told me sometimes they leave early," Shelby offers. "You know, when they migrate south? Maybe that's what happened."

I shake my head. Mr. Thurber would never leave this early. He doesn't take off until midway through September, and sometimes it's even later than that. And he'd never leave without saying good-bye. He always, always says good-bye.

"You sure?" Shelby sucks in her cheeks and spits a sunflower seed. It sails across the road and disappears inside a clump of blue cornflowers.

I nod. Definitely.

Jack kicks a pebble into a clump of grass nearby. "Pippa thinks she and Mr. Thurber have a special connection. Some kind of Animal Planet thing where she can understand what he's thinking."

I frown, glaring at my brother. It's not like him to make fun of me. Especially in front of someone he's trying to impress all the time.

"Well, maybe she does," Shelby says. "I knew a guy in Texas who could stare into a rattlesnake's eyes until it stopped rattlin' and slithered away in the other direction."

"Yeah, right." Jack kicks at another rock.

Shelby arches an eyebrow. "You don't believe me?"

Jack doesn't say anything but he doesn't have to. The expression on his face says it all.

Thankfully, the bus lumbers around the corner just then, before things get really uncomfortable. But not before I catch Shelby slitting her eyes at Jack. I know just how she feels. It stinks having someone you thought was in your corner act the way Jack's acting. I don't know what the problem is, but ever since the Middlebury trip with Dad, he's been acting weird.

And I'm going to find out why.

Chapter 22
JACK

It's been five days since Middlebury.

Dad and I haven't talked about it. Not once.

It's not that I haven't wanted to. I have. Especially after the story in the newspaper came out two days later. I grabbed the pages right out of Pippa's hands while she was reading it and walked out of the house. I had to sit down on the porch; my knees were buckling. Right on the back of the first page was a picture of Dad. It must've been taken from some kind of video camera in the corner of the bank. He was standing in front of the bank teller, and even though it was a little fuzzy, you could make out the Batman mask. You could see the collar of his dress shirt and the way his hair stuck out along the bottom of the mask.

SUPERVILLAIN ROBS BANK IN MIDDLEBURY, the headline reads. The article that followed said everything I already knew—minus any information about me. I know it sounds terrible, but I practically bawled when I realized no one had seen me. That I was—at least as far as I could tell—still safe.

I didn't even hear Pippa come up behind me, not until she stuck her little notebook over my shoulder and practically gave me a heart attack.

"What's the matter with you?" I bellowed, smacking away her notebook without bothering to look at what she'd written. "Don't you know better than to sneak up on people?" She looked stricken for a second, as if I had slapped her in the face, but I didn't care.

I took off, crushing the newspaper into a ball and throwing it into the garbage can by the mailbox. My bike was on the ground in front of the shed, and I snatched it up and started pedaling down Lake Road like a crazy person. The skin on my face was hot and my fingertips tingled. I rode and rode until my legs felt like rubber and my chest hurt from pulling in air.

And then, because there was nowhere else to go and nothing more I could do, I turned around and rode back home again.

I want to ask Dad about the police, about how long it might take for them to look for us, what things they'll dust for fingerprints, and how long they'll keep looking before they start working on something else.

And I want to ask him how much money he got, if it's enough to pay off the mortgage and catch up on the bills and give him time to find a real job so we can put this behind us and forget it ever happened.

But I can't bring myself to ask him anything. I guess I'm scared. I don't want to say the words out loud. If I hear them coming out of my mouth, the whole thing will have been real.

It will have actually happened.

And if it actually happened, that means I was there. Even if Dad and I are the only two people who know it.

It's hard to know how to feel about all of it. I'm so angry at Dad. But I don't know if I've ever felt this badly for him either. Take the night we came home from Middlebury and found Nibs sitting on our couch in the dark. Pippa was asleep next to her, so she kept her voice down, but even her whispers were loud.

"Why has your electricity been turned off, Sam?" she asked. "And the water, too. Did you know they're both off?"

"Jack." Dad nodded at me. "Take your sister upstairs, all right? Hit the sack. I'll see you in the morning."

I got Pippa tucked into bed, but I didn't go into my room. I sat on the stairs and listened. I didn't know about the water yet, but I wasn't surprised. Not really. Not with the way things were going. I'm not normally an eavesdropper, but there was no way I could sleep with everything that had just happened. My whole body felt like one big power line, twitching and buzzing with electricity.

I wanted to hear what Dad was going to tell Nibs. How he was going to explain it to her.

"I know it's none of my business," Nibs said softly. "And I don't mean to interfere with your personal business. Really I don't. But I'm worried about you, Sam. And the children. Pippa couldn't even brush her teeth tonight because the water's been shut off. Did you know that? There's no food in the refrigerator, and when I—"

Dad cut her off. "It's been a tough few months. Things have piled up, and I've gotten behind, obviously. But I just got a good chunk of money from the job in Middlebury. I can pay everything off now, so we'll be fine. Really. I appreciate your concern, Nibs, but you don't have to worry. I'm on it, okay? I really am."

And he was on it. When he came home the next day with groceries and all those new clothes from Murphy's, plus extra supplies for school, it felt good. It really did. And when the electricity and the water went back on, and I saw Dad mailing in mortgage payments to the bank, it felt even better. Like maybe the whole thing had sort of been worth it. That maybe it wasn't as bad as I'd made it out to be.

The night before school started, Dad went out and bought a whole bunch of steaks and grilled them up as a thank-you dinner for Nibs. She was thrilled. Actually, *tickled* was the word she kept using. "Well, this is completely unnecessary, but I'm tickled for you, Sam. Just tickled."

It was nice to see her happy, especially after she'd been so worried about us, and even nicer to see Dad standing up a little straighter and lifting his chin as she smiled. As if he'd been able to do something right, finally.

Even if he'd had to rob a bank to do it.

Chapter 23
PIPPA

Miss Rhonda Rhodes, my new teacher, is not pretty at all. She has short, scraggly blonde hair, a big mole on her cheek, and crooked teeth. I can't tell how old she is, but her brown skirt, baggy blue shirt, and soft white sneakers remind me of Grandma Kendall. To top it all off, she smells like Ritz crackers and old-lady perfume.

It's going to be a long year.

But there are other things to worry about right now aside from Miss Rhonda Rhodes. Like Molly and Susan, who are practically tripping over each other to get to my desk.

"Hey, Pippa," Molly says. "Didn't you see me waving at you in homeroom?" Molly has thick blonde hair and six freckles on her face. Every time I look at them, I think about connecting the dots. If I did, it would make a perfect box around her eyes, nose, and chin. Now I nod, staring at her belt, which is blue with little pink fish embroidered on it.

"And me, too?" Susan asks. Susan is the shortest girl in our class. Her hands are half the size of mine, and she still buys her shoes in the children's department.

I nod at Susan's question too and press my lips together.

Susan and Molly exchange a worried glance. "But you're not talking to us anymore?" Molly asks. "Like, at all?" Her face is squished up. She sounds hurt. Maybe even a little annoyed.

I don't want to pull out my notebook. I know the looks they'll give one another if I do, even though it's the only way right now that I could say I'd love to talk to them, but that I can't because all my words are trapped inside and I don't know how to get them out.

"My mom says we have to give her time," Susan half whispers, as if I'm not sitting right there and can't hear her. "You know, 'cause of everything that happened."

I glance up at Susan. I've always liked her. She's funny and she doesn't let the rude things other kids have said about being so small get her down. But right now, I want to punch her in the arm. Hard.

"All right everyone!" Miss Rhodes claps her hands. "Please take a seat. We need to get started!"

Molly catches my gaze and looks away quickly, grabbing Susan's arm. "Come on," she says. "Sit with me over here."

I watch them go, unable to look away as they settle themselves in a pair of desks against the wall. Maybe I *should* try the notebook with them. Would they laugh?

Think I'm too weird to stay friends with? Could I make it through the whole year without friends?

"All right, class," Miss Rhodes begins. "I'd like to start with the letter I mailed each of you at the beginning of the summer. Let's see a show of hands please. How many of you got that in the mail?"

A forest of hands appears, including mine, which I raise very slowly.

"And the book?" Miss Rhodes continues, arching an eyebrow. "*Tito the Warrior?*"

Another sea of hands.

"Wonderful!" Miss Rhodes claps her hands again. She has a high-pitched, scratchy voice. "Then I'd like everyone to get out the list of facts I asked you to make while reading your book." There is a flurry of movement as students reach down for folders and notebooks and place them on their desks. I don't move.

Miss Rhodes flicks her eyes over the class, pauses on me, and then moves on. "Who would like to start?"

Molly raises her hand. "When they were born, Spartan babies were inspected for any kind of physical problems," she reads from her notebook. "If the baby was sick, he was abandoned on a hillside, where he was left to die."

There is a murmur throughout the class, followed by nodding, knowing heads.

"That's exactly right, Molly." Miss Rhodes' voice has turned grave. "The Spartan culture was very, very strict. Any kind of weakness was not tolerated. And even if the babies did pass the first physical inspection, there were other challenges ahead. Would anyone like to comment on that?"

George Hayward, in the front row, raises his hand. "Yeah, they were still strict with the toddlers," he says, glancing at his notes. "They ignored them when they cried. And they taught the kids not to be afraid of the dark or of being alone. Like, if they could conquer those two things, they could pretty much do anything."

"Very good, George," Miss Rhodes says. "Now who can tell me what happened to the Spartan children when they reached the age of five?"

More hands.

I slink down farther and farther in my seat, pretending not to notice as Miss Rhodes glances at me and then looks away again. Gabby Richards informs the class that five-year-old Spartan children were taken away from their parents and sent to live in a gigantic house with other kids, where their military training began. Kayla Stevens tells everyone that Spartan military training was some of the most brutal ever recorded, and it included things like being whipped in public and going without food or warm clothing for long periods of time.

"Very, very good," Miss Rhodes says, surveying the class a final time. "Now after hearing all that, it might be hard to imagine why the Spartans treated children so harshly. It's because they wanted them to become brave, courageous soldiers. After overcoming so many challenges in their youth, heading into battle was nothing to these guys. And this leads me to our first class project. As we continue to study *Tito the Warrior* and Spartan culture, I want each of you to think about someone you might describe as a modern-day Spartan. They don't need to have endured the kind of childhood that Spartan kids did, of course, but they must have overcome some kind of difficulty that has made them into the brave, courageous person they are today. It can be a man, a woman, or even someone your own age. You are going to write a paper about this person and then present it to the class. We are also going to have a little ceremony on the day the papers are delivered, and you are encouraged to invite the person you wrote about to attend. We'll have a small reception afterward, with cake and punch. How does that sound?"

There is a combination of gasps and groans, clapping, and slumping against the desks.

I am one of the slumpers.

When the bell rings, Miss Rhodes calls my name. "Pippa? Will you come here please?"

I walk toward her slowly, wondering whether or not she saw me hiding from her. Or if I am going to have to use my notebook.

She smiles warmly at me as I approach and pats the chair next to her desk. "Have a seat."

I sit down. Pull on my earlobe.

"I'm friends with Mrs. Nivens," she says. "Nibs."

Some of the breath I'm holding releases itself, like air from a balloon.

"I know the past few months have been a very difficult time for you," Miss Rhodes says. "And it's perfectly okay if you don't want to talk to anyone right now. But please, Pippa"—she pauses, putting a hand on my arm—"please try to keep up with the work. If there's something that feels too hard to do, let me know and we'll figure it out together. But I don't want you to fall behind. I don't want to see you get left back because you were worried about asking for help." Her fingers tighten around my arm. "Okay?"

I look up. Her eyelids are covered in light blue eye shadow, which make her hazel eyes look green. I nod, sliding my arm out from under her hand, and give her a tiny smile. She's actually a lot nicer than she looks.

Maybe it won't be such a long year, after all.

Chapter 24
JACK

Ben's not in my homeroom, which normally would have bummed me out, since we've shared the same homeroom for the last four years, but now it fills me with a strange sort of relief. I don't need any more weird scenes between us than what's already going to come. Because I know it'll be strange. I know he's probably still mad at me for calling him an idiot and that he'll ignore me in the halls or pretend he doesn't know me when someone says my name. I don't need the added stress of being invisible. Not to Ben, who I thought would be my best friend for the rest of my life. Not right now.

But when I find out that I'm in Mr. Evans' homeroom, I get really bummed out, because Mr. Evans is bald and pudgy and seriously one of the weirdest people on the planet. He wears crazy ties that stop halfway down his shirt and belts with huge cowboy buckles. And he has this horrible habit of picking his nose when he thinks no one is looking and then flicking it under his desk. It's gross. It really is. Every time I leave his room, I feel like I need to take a shower.

But then Shelby walks in with her pink cowboy boots and white skirt. Everyone turns to stare at her, and I start to feel a tiny bit better about the situation because I know I already have a leg up on everyone else.

Then she sees me. Almost immediately, she turns around and heads for a desk on the other side of the room.

Great.

I knew I should have kept my mouth shut about that dumb rattlesnake guy at the bus stop. I don't know what's wrong with me. I really don't. I never would have been such a jerk like that in the past. Part of me still wants to impress her in the hopes that she'll like me. And then there's another part that doesn't care, because I know it wouldn't work anyway. Liking someone means spending time with them, talking on the phone, and finding out all their stuff. And if Shelby found out about my stuff—at least, the real stuff—she'd turn and run as fast as she could in the opposite direction.

Just like she did right now.

Ben's in our usual spot at lunch, sitting at the table near the cafeteria door. I catch sight of him as I come in, but he's shouting and laughing with Randy Plaska and Matt Piazza and John Davis, who are the three best players on the basketball team and are probably trying to recruit him to play this year. We're all in the same fourth period English class too. And now they do the exact thing to me that they did when I walked in there: nothing. None of them notice as I pass by. Not one of them looks up.

I'm not surprised that Ben's blowing me off, but I am annoyed that he seems to be getting tight with those other guys, who he's always considered a bunch of dorks. Ben's never been the sports type, but I wonder if they'll convince him to try out for basketball because of his height. Or because they can, now that I'm out of the picture.

But once I stop feeling annoyed, I start to feel nervous. I never used to have to worry about where to sit at lunch. I always just sat next to Ben. Every single day, for the last five years. Now, as I get closer to the end of the line, holding my tray, I can feel myself start to sweat. What am I going to do, go sit by myself in the corner like some loser? Head over to Ben's table and stand there, waiting for them to ask me to sit down? Slink away like a total moron when they don't?

This sucks.

And then I hear a voice from somewhere behind me. "Hey, Jack!"

I turn around. Shelby's leaning out of the line, straining to make eye contact. "Can I sit with you? Just for today? I don't really know . . ."

"Yeah, sure." I cut her off, trying to act all cool and casual, but my heart's beating a mile a minute. Maybe she's over the rattlesnake thing from this morning. "I'll wait for you down here."

She nods, giving me a thumbs-up. "Thanks."

I should be the one thanking her.

She doesn't even know that she just saved my life.

It's hard to sit for forty minutes across the table from someone who's so pretty and still remember to eat. It really is. Shelby's denim shirt makes her eyes look even greener, and up close I can see gold bursts inside the green, as if tiny suns have exploded behind her pupils. Silver earrings in the shape of S's gleam against her tan earlobes, and her teeth are as white as pieces of Chiclet gum. For as small as she is, she doesn't seem to have any issues with eating, either. Her tray is loaded with two grilled cheese sandwiches, a pile of French fries, creamed corn, two chocolate milks, and an Oreo cookie pudding sundae.

She digs right in, devouring a grilled cheese in less than two minutes, dipping the corners in a mixture of ketchup and mustard, and wiping her mouth with a napkin after each bite.

"Hey, listen," I say after a few minutes. "I'm sorry about giving you a hard time at the bus stop. About the rattlesnake guy and all. I didn't mean to be a jerk."

"You weren't a jerk," she says, still chewing. "I couldn't care less if you believe me or not."

Her answer sounds like a scolding, or worse, a brush-off, and I can feel a heat rising in my cheeks. I bend over my milk and pull on the straw. Laughter and shouts fill the room, and the heavy smells of melted cheese and butter hang in the air.

"Lunch is always the worst part of the day," Shelby says, coming up for air. "I hate lookin' for a place to sit."

"Tell me about it."

"Where are your friends?" She straightens up a little, looking around. "Don't you have a group you usually sit with?"

"Don't do that." I hunch down, nervous that Ben or his new crew has seen her glancing in their direction. I don't need any of them thinking that I'm talking about them. "Come on, just sit still."

"What're *you* so jumpy about?" Shelby shoves three fries into her mouth. "I thought you were popular here."

I give her a look. "Who told you that?"

"No one." She shrugs. "You just look like you would be."

I look like I'm popular? What does popular look like? What do I look like?

"Were you popular at your old school?" I ask.

Shelby rolls her eyes.

"No?"

"We have three groups of people at my old school." Shelby holds up three fingers. "Upper trash, middle trash,

162

and lower trash. I was lower trash. Prob'ly about as unpopular as you can get."

I don't know what Shelby is talking about, but I do know that I'd never put the word *trash* in the same sentence as her. She's about as far removed from trash as anyone I've ever known. "Well, you'll be popular here. Just give it a few days. You'll see."

"I better not be." She scoops a mouthful of creamed corn into her mouth, blotting her mouth again with the napkin. "I do better flying solo. I don't want any friends."

"Why not?"

"Waste of time. No point."

"What are you talking about?" I take a bite of my hamburger. "Everyone wants friends."

"I'm not everyone." She pulls on her straw, watching me with her green eyes.

"What about Pippa and me?" I point out. "We're your friends."

"That's what you think."

"We're not?" I push down a flash of annoyance. Who *is* this girl?

"You're just people I know," Shelby answers. "Who happen to live near my aunt and uncle."

"That's all?"

"That's all." She wipes her mouth a final time and stands up from the table. Every last morsel on her tray is gone.

"Why'd you want me to sit with you, then?" I ask quickly. "I mean, if you don't care about having friends?"

"You don't have to be friends with someone to have a conversation with them," she answers. "It's nice to eat and talk, don't you think?"

She's the strangest girl I've ever met, I think as I watch her walk away. *Weird, even.*

So why does that make me like her even more?

Chapter 25
PIPPA

One day, a few months after we found out that Mom had cancer, she pointed to the movie marquee as we drove past the mall. "There's that goofy movie you've been wanting to see," she said. "*Fat Dog Takes the Cake?*"

I looked out the window and pretended not to hear her. We had just left a store that sold wigs, and Mom's new one was in a hatbox in the backseat. She hadn't lost all her hair yet, but the little she had left clung to her scalp in strange, wispy little patches. Still, I thought the wig, which the saleswoman had told her was an "adorable pixie cut," looked even worse than her missing hair. It was a dull brown color and chopped in short, raggedy layers. I bit my lip when she first put it on and tried not to cry. It made her look like a stranger. But when Mom turned around and asked me what I thought, I smiled and told her it was cute. I was afraid not to.

A few days earlier, she and I had been arguing about something, and I stormed off the way I used to do whenever I didn't get my way. I slammed the door to my room and plunked down on my bed. Two seconds later, Jack walked in. I raised my head, ready to yell at him too, and then changed my mind. Something about the look on his face stopped me.

"*What?*" I asked instead.

"You know she's not going to make it out of this, don't you?" His voice was quiet. Dangerously quiet. And his lower lip was quivering. I just lay there, holding myself up on my elbows, and stared at him. "She doesn't have a lot of time left, Pip. You might want to spend the rest of it being nice to her." And then he turned around and walked out of my room.

I still didn't know whether or not I believed him, but I did make up my mind right then and there that I wouldn't say another bratty or unkind thing to Mom again. Ever. Which was why I lied about the wig. And why, when she asked me about the movie, I knew I would lie again.

"That's the one, isn't it, Pip?" she pressed. "You've been talking about it for months. Are you going to go see it with Molly and Susan?"

I nodded, although I knew I wouldn't. Molly and Susan had called a few days earlier and asked me to go, but I lied to them too, making up some dumb story about being grounded. The truth was, I couldn't think of anything worse than sitting in a theater laughing at some stupid dog, while my mom was at home with cancer. And in a horrible-looking wig, to boot.

"You think they'd be mad if I took you first?" Mom asked. "How about it? You want to go right now, just you and me?"

I shook my head again, although I couldn't think of anything I wanted to do more, and pressed my fingertips against the corners of my eyes. Sometimes that kept the tears away.

Mom pulled the car over on the shoulder of the highway. She waited for a moment, just sitting there, but I still didn't turn around. I couldn't. Every time I looked at her now, I started to cry, thinking about what Jack had said, and how much I was going to miss her. She reached out finally and stroked my hair. "Oh Pippa, honey, I know it's hard. You won't ever know how badly I want to stay here with you. Trying to accept that I can't has been the hardest battle of my entire life. But I'm here now, honey."

I moved my head a few inches toward her.

"I'm still right here."

Another inch.

"Will you go see that movie with me?" she asked. "So we can laugh our heads off at how ridiculous it is and stuff ourselves with chocolate chip cookie dough bites and popcorn?"

I didn't answer. I couldn't. My face was buried against the folds of her blue gingham shirt, breathing in her rubbing-alcohol-and-hospital smell, and feeling the curve of her arms around my back.

The movie was the dumbest one I'd ever seen. But sitting there in the darkened theater, holding Mom's hand and listening to her laugh, turned it into one of the best days of my life.

That's what I think about sitting out on the dock the next morning, waiting for the sky to split in two. How Mom and I laughed and laughed that day. I can't even remember what it feels like to laugh anymore.

Nibs' footsteps sound behind me. "You're up even earlier than me this morning," she says, handing me a mug of chai. "Back-to-school jitters?"

I take the mug and shrug a little.

She sits down next to me, placing the folded newspaper between us, and takes a sip from her own mug. "Well, I'm dying to know. What'd you think of Miss Rhodes?"

I nod my approval, give her a thumbs-up.

"Oh, I'm glad," Nibs says. "She's a gem, that one. Heart of gold. I've known her forever. We started teaching together actually, back in 1984." She elbows me gently. "We're a couple of dinosaurs." She sips again from her drink and balances her mug on her knee. "I hope you don't mind that she told me you hadn't done any of the work she assigned over the summer. You know you can come to me if you need help."

My embarrassment turns quickly to annoyance. I know Nibs is trying to help, but I don't need her babysitting me. She did her part, which I'm thankful for, but now she needs to back off and let me do mine. I slide my notebook out from inside Mom's sweater pocket and write.

"**No babysitting!**" Nibs reads aloud, nodding. "Okay, that's fair." She watches as I write some more and then reads my words again: "**Besides, I've already thought about who I am going to do my Spartan paper on.**"

I hadn't realized it until just this moment. But it's so obvious that I've got to do it on Mom. *Trying to accept that I can't be with you has been the hardest battle of my life.* She even used the word *battle*! And I've never known anyone as brave and courageous as she was. Ever. Anywhere.

"Well, that's excellent news," Nibs says, ruffling the top of my head. "I'm very glad to hear it." She gives me a wink as she shakes open the paper and starts reading.

I look out at the lake as Nibs loses herself in the day's news. A thread of excitement shoots through me as I think about the essay. About comparing Mom to a Spartan warrior. It will be great. It will be—

"Unbelievable," Nibs murmurs, shaking her head.

I glance over her shoulder to see what she's reading. **POLICE SAY SUPERVILLAIN HAS STRUCK BEFORE**, the headline blares.

"Can you believe this moron?" Nibs snorts. "They're saying he tried to rob a bank in Rutland a few months back wearing a Spider-Man mask, but he chickened out and ran off before he could get the money. Then just last week he showed up at a bank in Middlebury wearing a Batman mask and made off with three thousand five hundred dollars."

A faint alarm goes off in the back of my head as Nibs shakes her head again. "People are crazy," she says. "Absolutely, unequivocally bonkers."

This time, for some reason, the alarm feels a little bit closer.

It sounds a little bit louder.

As if whatever—or whoever—is ringing it is not very far away at all.

Chapter 26
JACK

Day Two of school doesn't feel as long as Day One. Maybe because Ben passes the ball to me at gym, even though the rest of the day slips by without another glance. Or maybe it's because I eat lunch again with Shelby who, true to her word, ignores everyone who looks her way or calls her name (which, two days in, happens more often than she'd want to admit).

She looks almost prettier than yesterday, dressed in a lemon-colored shirt with little ruffles in the front and dark jeans tucked inside her pink cowboy boots. But man, it's hard to figure her out. She's not a giggly kind of girl. She's definitely not Alice Jamison.

"You get any books yet?" I ask.

"Of course." She takes a huge bite of pizza and chews, dabbing at her mouth again with her napkin. "My teachers couldn't wait to give them to me."

I glance down at the space under her seat, but there's nothing there. "So where are they?"

"In my locker, where they'll stay for the rest of the year."

"You're not going to use them?" I stop chewing. "At all?"

"I'll probably pull them out when the teachers start givin' me grief. But not until then."

"Why?"

"Why what?" she asks.

"Why wouldn't you use them? I mean, it sounds like you're just setting yourself up to fail."

She shrugs. "Maybe I am."

"You don't care if you fail?"

"I said maybe," she answers.

I take another bite of my sandwich. She has an unnerving ability to end a conversation by some of the things she says. And I'm never sure what to do next when it happens.

"Tell me about your mom," she says, swirling a tater tot in a puddle of ketchup and mustard. "I mean, if you want," she adds hurriedly, seeing the startled look on my face. "If it's not . . . you know . . . too hard."

It's the first time I've seen her ruffled. And I'm not sure why, but seeing that little crack in her tough-girl exterior makes me forget the directness of her question or the flash of panic that comes from hearing it. "What do you want to know?"

"Well . . . what'd she look like?"

My chewing slows as a picture of Mom in her hospital bed comes into my head, but I push past it and think about what she looked like before that. Way back, before she got sick. "She was pretty. Really pretty. Kinda tall. Long, dark hair. She was always twirling a piece of it. You know, like around her fingers." I pause, tapping my two front teeth. "She had a tooth right here in the front that crossed over the other one. She was embarrassed about it. She said it made her feel like she had buck teeth, and she always covered her mouth when she laughed. But I liked it. I thought it made her even prettier." I shrug and look down at my food. I feel like I've said too much, which is weird, because I hadn't been planning on saying anything at all.

"Did she work?" Shelby asks.

"She was a waitress. At the Rocking Robin here in town. Everyone liked her. People used to ask for her when they went in because she was so nice. And funny. She always made everyone laugh."

"That's nice." Shelby's voice is soft, but a detached look comes into her eyes, and I can tell she's thinking about something else. "I can't remember the last time my momma laughed at anything."

"No?"

Shelby shakes her head. "She hardly even smiles."

"Why not?"

"I don't know, really. I used to think it was because she drinks so much, but now I'm not sure."

I don't know what to say to that, so I don't say anything at all.

Shelby stares down at her tray. "I told Nibs and Pippa I was here because my parents were getting a divorce, but that wasn't really true. I just didn't want to get into all the details." She looks back up at me. "I'm mostly here, I guess, so's my mother can try to get her act together."

"You guess?" I echo. "You mean you're not really sure?"

" 'Course I'm sure." She sounds insulted for some reason, although that's the last thing I meant to do. "It's just . . ." She shrugs, shaking her head a little. "There's a lot more to it than that."

I want to ask her what "a lot more to it" means, but I don't want her to think I'm prying either. "What about your dad?" I ask instead. "Can he help her out at all, down there?"

"Nah. He's not around at all. He got tired of her drinkin' all the time and hit the road when I was in third grade. Haven't seen him since."

I stop chewing. The phrase *I'm sorry* springs to my lips and I swallow it.

"You haven't seen him since third grade? Like, not even once?"

Shelby shakes her head without looking at me. "Nope."

"Why not?"

She tosses the last of her pizza in her mouth, balls up her napkin, and looks me directly in the eye. "He's got better things to do I guess."

Her casualness makes me uneasy. It's hard to know if she doesn't care that her father doesn't speak to her or if she's lying through her teeth. Either way, I can't hold her gaze. I stare at the pile of potato chips on my tray, wondering if I should offer her one. Everything on her tray is already gone.

She stands up, beating me to the punch. "Well, thanks for the conversation." She takes a few steps and then turns around. "I wish I could've met your mom. She sounds cool."

And just like that, she's gone.

I head up to the tree house after school. There's still a ton of work that needs to be done. Half the roof is missing, the window in the back is crooked, and six of the nails in the wall have fallen out. But I lie down on the floor and stare up at the pocket of sky that peeks in through the leaves. I don't have the energy to do anything. Or maybe it's that I just don't want to. For the first time in my life, the tree house feels childish. Like something a little kid would spend time on. Not someone who will turn thirteen in three more months. Definitely not someone who was involved in a bank robbery.

I was involved, wasn't I? If the police came and demanded to know why I was there, I would have to tell them, right? No, sir, it wasn't just some coincidence that I was there. Yes, the prime suspect was my father. No, I wasn't standing guard, hanging out there in the foyer. Yes, I freaked out in the car and ran inside to make sure he was okay. Yes, I witnessed everything that happened. Yes, I left with him.

All these things make me an accomplice. That's what I am now. An accomplice to a bank robbery.

"Jack?" I sit up straight as Dad's voice floats up the trunk of the tree.

"Yeah?" I stick my head out the window and look down. He's already climbing the ladder, hand over hand, grimacing from the effort. My heart drops. He never comes up here unless he wants to talk. Except for *hi* and *bye* and *yeah* and *'night*, it'll be the first time we've talked in over a week. I slink back inside the tree house, press myself up tight against the wall. I don't want to talk. I'm still not ready.

Dad reaches the top and hauls himself inside. "Whew!" he says. "Haven't done that in a while."

I scratch one of my knees, hoping I don't look as scared as I feel. What's happened to me? How can I be scared of Dad?

He sits opposite me, both hands resting on top of his tented knees, and exhales loudly. He looks at me for a long moment. "How are you, buddy?"

I shrug.

"Yeah," he says softly. "That's sort of how I feel, too. Actually, that's why I came up here. Is there anything you want to ask me? Anything you want to talk about?"

I rub my chin, glance quickly at him, and then look away again.

"I know you do," Dad says encouragingly. "Just throw one out there. Anything at all."

I stare at the little space between my feet, my eyes trailing over a sliver of wood poking out of the smooth wooden floor. I move the tip of my toe over it, trying to press it down flat, but it doesn't budge. It's stuck there, glued rigidly with tree sap, hard as a nail.

"Jack."

"What if we get caught?" I blurt out. "Your picture was in the paper, you know."

"I saw that," Dad answers. "But it was just footage from a video camera. And it was just my back. No one knows it was me."

"Pippa was reading the article," I continue, feeling something rise inside. *"Pippa!"*

"Pippa reads Nibs' paper every morning, buddy." Dad lowers his knees. "She doesn't know. Trust me, okay? She doesn't know anything."

I bring a hand to my forehead to push my hair out of my face. It's shaking. My whole body is shaking. It's exactly like I thought. Saying it out loud is making it real. And making it real is too much.

"What're you doing now?" I can hear the accusation in my voice, but I don't care. "I mean, when we're in school? Are you out looking for a job?"

"Yes," Dad says. "I've put a whole bunch of resumes out at different places. We'll see what happens. These things take time, you know."

The shaking slows a little, hearing this. Sending out resumes is definitely a step in the right direction. Someone will call him soon for an interview and he'll go in and answer the questions he needs to answer and get a job and everything will go back to normal. "How much time?" I ask.

Dad shrugs. "Hard to tell. Although I really don't have a lot of time to play around with. You know, I only came away with three thousand five hundred dollars." He wipes his forehead with the back of his hand. "I couldn't believe it when I counted it all out. I thought I'd gotten at least two or three times that amount. And I know three thousand five hundred dollars sounds like a lot of money, but it isn't going to go very far."

Somehow, I find my voice. "That's what your new job is for."

Dad flashes me a smile, and when he does, something inside of me crumbles, because it's one of those fake, tight smiles that says he's hiding something. "Right?" I press, pretending I haven't seen it, that everything is still okay.

"Of course." He nods. "I mean, that's the plan."

"'That's the plan?'" I echo. "What does that even mean?"

"Listen, Jack," Dad says. "We're just going to have to take things as they come. I'm looking hard for a job and I will keep on doing that. I promise you. But if we run out of money again before that happens . . ." He pauses, scratching his head. "I mean, if there's a chance of losing your mother's house again . . ."

He doesn't say it out loud. He doesn't have to.

"But I'm getting ahead of myself. Way, way ahead of myself." He looks around the little room, as if seeing it for the first time. "Wow, it looks great up here buddy, you know that? Really great."

But his words sound empty. He's just saying them to try to fill a space between us that nothing in the whole entire world will ever be able to fill again.

Chapter 27
PIPPA

I don't know what the ringing in my head means. I'm pretty sure it's ringing for a reason, but I can't figure it out. It's like the connect-the-dot freckles on Molly's face; I can see the box around them, but only in my imagination, not because it's actually there. Still, I get a weird feeling when I hear Nibs read that article on the dock, especially when she says the words *Spider-Man* and *Middlebury* and *Batman*. I think about them all day in school, as they hit and bounce off each other like one of those metal balls in a pinball machine. I have a feeling that they're all connected in some way, but I still don't know how.

So it's sort of like I'm watching myself from the outside when I walk over to Dad's blue Eldorado later that day and open the door. I don't even know what I'm looking for, really. But maybe I'll be able to figure it out when I find it. Jack's in the tree house and Dad's gone upstairs to nap, so neither of them will notice me. Neither of them will care.

It smells like old French fries inside the car. An empty bottle of water has been crammed in between the driver's seat and the clutch, and a pile of loose change sits in a small paper cup under the dashboard. I look in the back, lifting up the floor mats and peeking under the dark wedge of seats, but nothing stands out. Whatever it is I'm looking for, it isn't there.

Then I remember the trunk.

I wish I didn't know how to pop a trunk, but I do. Dad showed me a few years ago, after Molly came over one day and hid there during a game of hide-and-seek, and I ran screaming to him because I didn't know how to get her out. He was furious, but it was the kind of mad that had more to do with being scared than being angry. It was easy to get stuck in a trunk, he told us. And dangerous, too. He took Molly and me over to the front of the car and showed us the lever by the door that popped it open. "Stay away from car trunks as a general rule," he said. "But if you ever need to get it open, pull this lever. You'll never get stuck if you know how to open the back of a car."

Now, I reach in on the driver's side of the car and pull the lever. The trunk bounces open and then drops again, staying slightly ajar. My heart is pounding so hard I can hear it in my ears, and the inside of my mouth tastes sour. I stare for a long time at the thin space between the lid and the bumper.

It's so dark.

Anything could be in there.

I lean forward, close my eyes, and lift it all the way open.

———————————

I don't mean to scare Jack, but when he catches sight of me hiding behind his bedroom door, he jumps so far back that he bumps his head on the wall.

"What the heck, Pippa?" He rubs the back of his head with one hand and grabs my arm with the other. "Get out of my room!"

A high-pitched noise comes out of my throat as he drags me toward the door, and I lean back, reaching for the Batman mask on the floor.

Jack freezes when he sees the mask, and he lets go of my arm.

"What's going on in there?" Dad's voice drifts down the hall. "Everyone all right?"

Jack leans over slowly, like he's moving in slow motion, and picks up the mask.

"Jack? Pippa?"

"We're fine, Dad!" Jack's voice cracks on the second word. He strides over to the door and shuts it carefully, still holding the mask in his hand. Then he turns around and stares at me with huge eyes. "Where'd you get this?"

I take a step back, frightened.

Jack yanks me by the wrist again. "Where'd you *get* this, Pippa?" His hand is too tight and I scrunch my eyes up and whimper. "Shhhh!" he says fiercely, dragging me toward the bed. But his hand loosens a little, and his voice gets softer. "Sit down, okay? Just sit down for a minute." The meanness in his voice is fading. He arranges himself across from me on the mattress and crosses his legs. "Pippa," he says. "This is important, okay? I really, *really* need you to talk to me right now. Do you have your notebook?"

I nod.

"Can you use it?"

I nod again.

"Okay." He pauses, waiting. "Get it out, then."

I pull the notebook and my pink glitter pen out of my back pocket, not taking my eyes off him, not sure what he's going to do next.

"Where'd you find this?" Jack shakes the mask again in his hand.

"In the trunk of Dad's car."

Jack reads my answer and looks at something on the wall behind me. His forehead is all wrinkled up, like he's trying to remember something. "What were you doing looking around in Dad's trunk?" he asks finally.

I shrug. I don't know how to describe the alarm in my head after I heard Nibs read the newspaper article on the dock, or why I went looking for something I didn't know I would find.

"Did you see anything else?"

I nod.

"What, Pippa? Write it down!"

"Pillowcase."

Jack's eyes flit over the word and he looks back up. "Anything else?"

I nod and bend over my notebook. "But not in Dad's car."

"What do you mean?"

Jack's knee starts jiggling as I write again. "I found your Spider-Man mask," he reads slowly. "On the living room floor. The night you left. For Middlebury."

"Spider-Man mask?" He looks confused. "But . . . I don't . . ." He gets up off the bed and starts walking around his room. There are T-shirts and shorts and underwear all over the place, but he walks right on top of them.

"The paper said Spider-Man tried to rob a bank in Rutland," I write, tapping on my notebook to get his attention. "Last month. But then he got scared and ran away."

Jack walks back over and reads my words. His eyebrows narrow. "What are you talking about? What paper? When? When did you see this?"

I gesture with my hand for him to follow me, and we head downstairs to the kitchen. The article about the curly-haired woman catching the huge catfish on Lake Bomoseen is still on the front of the refrigerator, held in place with a blue stone magnet. When I point to it, Jack snatches it off the refrigerator. The magnet goes flying, skittering across the floor like a rock. "This is about a fish, Pippa!"

He clenches his jaw as I turn the paper over in his hands. I watch him the whole time he reads, his eyes flying back and forth across the article like ticker tape, and when I know he's gotten to the end, I curl my index finger around one of his belt loops. But he grabs me around the wrist and pulls me back upstairs. I stumble alongside him, trying not to fall. Inside his room, he lets me go and shuts the door.

"What's happening, Jack?" I write quickly. "I'm scared."

"Just hold on, okay?" He folds the article in half and shoves it inside one of his pockets. "Just hold on and let me think." He runs both hands through his hair and locks his fingers around the back of his head.

"You don't have to be scared." His voice sounds hollow. "It's going to be okay."

"What is?"

"I don't know." He lets his hands drop heavily. "Everything, I guess."

"What happened in Middlebury?"

Jack swallows when he reads my question and then walks away.

I write again and get up off the bed, pushing the notebook in his face. "I want to know what's going on!!!"

Jack's face gets red when he reads this and he snatches the book out of my hands. "Listen to me," he says in a dead-quiet voice. "Whatever you're thinking, it's not true. So just leave it alone, okay? I mean it, Pippa. Leave it alone."

I reach for my book, but he holds it up over my head, out of reach. And then, without warning, he flings it across the room. My little pink book hits the wall and drops down into a pile of blankets like a big, dead insect. I turn around, furious, ready to smack him, but he's already disappeared.

The sound of heavy footsteps thuds down the stairs, and by the time I race to the window to see where he's gone, all I can make out is the little red reflector on the back of his bike as it flies down Lake Road.

Chapter 28
JACK

It's dark outside. The kind of night where you can barely see your hand in front of your face. But I don't care. I could ride Lake Road blindfolded by now, I've done it so many times. My legs know every twist and turn by heart, and my hands can steer this bike in my sleep. Besides, I don't want to see anything right now. I just want to ride. And ride. And ride.

I can't believe I didn't know about the bank in Rutland. It must have been Dad. It had to have been, with the Spider-Man mask and the note; it's almost identical to how everything went down in Middlebury. Maybe that's why he wanted me to come with him. So it wouldn't feel quite so scary the second time. So he wouldn't chicken out and run off again.

And now Pippa knows.

PIPPA KNOWS!

By the time the two words scream through my head a final time, I can't breathe, no matter how hard I try. I jump off my bike, letting it roll wildly and crash into the bushes along the side of the road. When I lean over, grabbing my knees, every single curse word I know comes pouring into my head. And before I know what's happening, they're pouring out of my mouth, too. I probably shouldn't know as many curse words as I do, but Ben's dad swears like a sailor, and last summer when I spent almost every day over there, I learned a lot of them. Bad ones, too. The kind of bad that Mom would wash my mouth out with soap if she heard me say. Maybe even worse than that.

But I don't care. They shoot out of my mouth like a stream of fireworks, and I'm kicking rocks and picking up sticks and throwing them as hard as I can into the dark. And then, all of a sudden, I'm crying. My legs give out from under me, and I sort of collapse in a heap on the side of the road and just bawl my eyes out.

I don't know if I've ever felt so scared in my whole life.

I don't know if I've ever missed Mom more than this moment.

I don't know if I know anything anymore.

After a while, I sit back up and wipe my nose on the bottom of my T-shirt. I pull my bike out of the weeds and tear out the strands of honeysuckle vine that have gotten caught in the wheels. I don't feel like getting back on it. My legs still feel rubbery and my head is pounding. I walk beside it instead, holding the handlebars with one hand so it doesn't fall over and closing my eyes every few seconds to ward off the ache behind them.

I don't want to go home, but I've been gone longer than an hour and Dad has rules about being out too late, which means he'll probably come looking for me if I'm gone too long. Besides, Pippa will probably get herself all worked up, worrying where I am. But then I see a yellow beam, like a flashlight, and a pair of pink boots dangling over one side of Finster's Rock.

"Shelby?" I whisper.

She sits up quickly, wiping at her face. "What're you doing here?"

"I was just out riding my bike. Are you okay?"

She sniffs through her clogged nose. "Yeah, I'm fine."

"Are you crying?"

"Yeah. So? People cry, you know."

"Not unless something's wrong, usually."

"Yeah, well." She waves me off. "Nothin's wrong with me, so I don't know what to tell you."

I stand there like an idiot for a minute, not sure what else to say. Should I leave her alone or ask her if she wants to talk? I'm not sure I would have wanted to talk if someone had found me a little while ago.

"Okay." I back my bike up and swing my leg over the seat. "Well, I hope you feel better."

"Who says I was feelin' bad?"

Man, she's weird. "All right, see you around."

And then, just as I lean on the pedal and push the bike forward, she says my name. "Jack."

I look up. "What?"

"Don't go." Her voice is a whisper. "Please."

Chapter 29
PIPPA

"Hey, guys?" Dad's voice calls from out in the hall, but I don't move. I'm still in Jack's room, sitting on his bed, holding my little pink notebook. "I heard the front door slam." Dad pokes his head into Jack's room and frowns when he sees me. "Honey? What are you doing in here? Is everything okay?"

I want to ask him the same question. But Jack already told me it would be all right, and I don't believe him, either.

"Pippa?" Dad comes into the room slowly and before I know what I'm doing, I'm off the bed and racing toward him. He catches me in both arms as I rest my head against his shoulder. "What's going on, honey? Did you and Jack have a fight?"

I nod my head as he rubs my back and try not to think about the Spider-Man or Batman masks. His hand goes around and around in little circles between my shoulders, just like he used to do to tuck me in when I was really little. "Oh honey, it's okay. It'll be all right."

I squeeze my eyes against the tears.

I love him so much.

No matter what, I will always love him so much.

━━━━━━━━━━━━━━━━━━━━

But I can't stop worrying about Jack. It's been almost two hours since he left. Dad's downstairs in the living room, watching TV and waiting up for him. Dad's going to read him the riot act when he gets home, maybe even ground him for a week, although neither of us have been grounded since Mom died. Still, Dad's pretty strict when it comes to being out alone at night. He's told us tons of times about the skunks and raccoons that come out looking for food, and there's always a chance one of them could be rabid. One bite by a rabid animal and you're done. Or at least you have to go to the hospital and get a whole bunch of shots.

I try not to think about being grounded or rabid animals when I open my bedroom window a few minutes later, scoot out onto the roof, and monkey-swing my way down the water pipe. But I overshoot the distance the bottom of the pipe is to the ground, and when I let go, I land with a loud thud. The flashlight tucked in the waistband of my shorts tumbles out and rolls to one side. For a moment, I just sit there, frozen, waiting for Dad to come charging out of the front door. But a few seconds pass and nothing happens. I count to thirty. Then sixty. Finally, I stand back up, grab my flashlight, and race across the lawn for my bike.

I've never been out on the lake this late. I had no idea it was so dark. Even with the flashlight, which I hold with one hand while trying to steer with the other, it looks like I'm moving inside a wall of tar. The darkest dark I can ever imagine. To keep my mind off being scared, I try to think of my favorite songs, but the only one that comes is one Mom used to sing to me when we would work in the garden together:

> *I plant my seeds*
> *I plant them row by row.*
> *I am a happy farmer*
> *And I like to see things grow!*
> *The sun and rain*
> *Are happy helpers too;*
> *They know that I*
> *Have lots of work to do*
> *So they just keep on helping out*
> *'Til everything is through.*

It's a dumb little song, but it makes me feel better, and I sing it in my head six times before I finally reach Jack's favorite fishing spot by the quarry.

But he's not there. I look around for ten minutes, shining my flashlight in every crack and crevice I can think of, but there's no sign of him. Where else would he have gone? Ben lives almost twenty minutes away, and I don't think they're even talking anymore. He wouldn't go into Poultney, would he? No, it's too far. Besides, there's no one in Poultney that he'd go see.

I try not to panic as I get back on my bike and start home again, but it's hard not to. Everything feels so crazy and uncertain right now. There's just no way to know what's going to happen. Jack didn't give me any real answers, but I have an awful feeling I already know what they are.

But what if I'm wrong? What if the alarm bells in my head and the words in the paper and even Jack's reaction to seeing the Batman mask I found are things I've gotten horribly, terribly wrong? I have to fight back tears, thinking of it.

Just as I'm coasting past Finster's Rock, I hear voices. My heart skips a beat as I realize that one of them is Jack's, and I turn around quickly, parking my bike against a tree.

"You're the one who asked me to stay." Jack sounds irritated. "And now you're telling me that I'm bothering you?"

"I didn't ask you to stay so you could ask me ten million questions!" I slide in behind a tree, listening to Shelby argue with my brother. "I asked you to stay because . . ."

"Because what?" Jack interrupts. "Because you wanted another lunch buddy? You wanted some dumb conversation with someone who's not your friend?"

Shelby doesn't answer right away and I bite my lip, looking around carefully for another place to hide in case Jack comes barreling out to the road again. He'll kill me if he knows I'm here.

And that I can hear every word they're saying.

Chapter 30
JACK

"I guess I have been a little bit of a jerk about things," Shelby says softly. "I'm sorry."

"You don't have to apologize." I cross my legs, trying to get comfortable on the rock. "I get it, believe me. My life sucks right now, too."

The corner of Shelby's mouth lifts up, and for the first time since I've met her, I feel like I've said something right.

"You know, when I first got here, my aunt and uncle's stove was on fire, so Nibs had to come pick me up at the airport," she says. "We got to talkin' a little bit, and she told me that there wasn't any point frettin' about the things I'd left behind. She said that the only thing I had to worry about was right here, right now. But I'll tell you what, sometimes right here right now can really suck too, can't it?"

"Yup."

She shrugs, digging inside her pocket and withdrawing a bag of sunflower seeds. "You want some?"

I shake my head, watching her chew out of the corner of her mouth and then pucker her lips. *Thwoot!* A faint splash sounds out on the lake. "You're pretty good at that, you know."

"I should be," Shelby answers. "I've been doin' it since I was five years old."

"Wow, really?"

"Mmm hmmm. My Pops taught me. He used to draw a line in the dirt a little ways from our front porch and make me practice hittin' it when I spit. Every time I did, he'd scrub out the line and draw another one farther away."

"So how far can you spit?"

"The farthest I ever measured was sixty feet. Give or take."

"Sixty feet?" I try not to sputter. "Holy cow! I can't even spit *six* feet!"

"I've been doin' it longer'n you."

"That's insane." I whistle softly. For a moment, neither of us says anything. The only sounds are the branches overhead stirring in the breeze and the soft murmur of the water below.

"You miss him?" I ask after another minute.

"Every second of every day." Shelby's answer comes so quickly that I wonder if it was already sitting there on the tip of her tongue.

"That's how I feel about my mom," I offer.

"What happened to her?" Shelby asks.

"She had stomach cancer." My throat tightens. "By the time they found out, she only had two months left. It was fast."

"You get to say good-bye?"

"Kinda." I reach up, scratch my nose, which has started tingling. "I mean, she'd said her last things, I guess. You know, like I love you and take care of Dad and Pippa and all that, and I got to tell her some things too, but I wasn't there when she actually *died* died."

"Where were you?"

"Pippa and I were outside in the hall actually, arguing."

"About what?"

"It was stupid. She was pestering my mom, asking her the same questions that she asked her every day. 'Why can't they fix you? Does anything hurt? Where's your medicine?' All this stuff, just over and over. I don't know why she kept doing it; I mean, my mom had already answered everything like ten million times. So when the nurse said that Mom needed to rest that day and asked us to go wait in the hall, I kind of went off on her and told her to shut up, that all her questions were driving Mom nuts, and while we were in the hall arguing, Mom died." I drop my head so that she doesn't see me wiggling my nose. "That was the last time Pippa said anything."

"Wow," Shelby says softly.

"Yeah."

"But it's not *your* fault that she stopped talking," Shelby says. "I mean, she just sorta did that on her own, right?"

"No, I should've never said anything like that to her. I should've just kept my dumb mouth shut."

"You were frustrated."

"Yeah. But I didn't have to be mean. I didn't have to say *that*."

"I didn't get to see my dad 'fore he left," Shelby says suddenly.

"You didn't?"

"He just left me a note. I didn't even know he was going anywhere."

"What'd the note say?"

Shelby gets that faraway look in her eyes again, and for a minute I don't think she's going to answer.

"I tore it up," she says softly.

"Oh."

"But I remember what it says." She nods. "I remember every word."

"You do?"

"*Dear Butterbean*," she starts, and then looks up. "That's what he called me all the time. Butterbean. You ever hear of 'em?" She shrugs when I shake my head no. "They're a Southern thing, mostly. Kind of like lima beans. They don't taste like much unless you put lots of butter and salt on them."

"Oh."

"*Dear Butterbean,*" she starts again, "*I don't know of two unhappier people than your Momma and me. We've tried just about everything to make things work between us, but it isn't going to happen. At least, not in this lifetime.*

"*You know how I've always told you that life is short? Well, it's even shorter when half of it has already passed you by. So I'm heading out West for a while. I need to see if I can find some kind of happy while I still have something left in me.*

"*I wanted to wait so that I could say good-bye to you in person, but my train will be leaving while you're at school. Take good care of yourself, you hear? I'll be back soon.*

"*Love, Pops.*"

She looks up at me as she says the last word, and then drops her eyes again. I don't know what to say. If I were her, I'd never want to memorize those words. I'd never want to repeat them. They're awful. Every single one of them. I can't imagine Mom or Dad ever feeling badly enough that they'd purposely leave us behind to go look for something else. And there's no way that they wouldn't say good-bye if one of them did have to go. I've never met Shelby's father, but I know I don't want to. Not in this lifetime.

"How long ago was that?" I ask finally.

"Four years," Shelby says. "I was just starting third grade."

"And you haven't heard from him since?"

Shelby shakes her head.

"Nothing?"

"Not one word."

"Then why'd he write 'I'll be back soon'?"

"Because parents *lie*." Shelby turns on me in a flash. "Don't you know that by now, Jack? They all lie, even the good ones, because they think that we can't handle hearin' the truth. But they're wrong. If my Pops had just come right out and written somethin' like, 'Listen, Butterbean, I love you, but I gotta go. I don't think we'll cross paths again for a good long while, and I'm sorry for that, but that's just the way it's gotta be'—if he had just written that, I'd be sad, sure, but I wouldn't be walkin' around like I do, still waitin' and prayin' for a miracle. I wouldn't be runnin' to the mailbox every day, lookin' for a letter from him, and my heart wouldn't be jumpin' outta my chest every time the phone rings."

I stare at her with new eyes, imagining her inside the Andersons' house, biting her lip when the phone rings, peering out from behind the front curtain as the mailman comes and leaves again. "That's what it's like?" I whisper.

"Yes!" she whispers fiercely. "And even though I know better, I can't make myself stop." Her eyes fill with tears. "I want so much to be wrong about him. I want so much to believe that he'll come back."

I don't know what to say. But I can't help thinking about Dad as she sits there, crying in the dark.

I want so much to be wrong about him.

I want so much to believe that he'll come back, too.

Chapter 31
PIPPA

I know it's hard for Shelby with the way things are for her. It can't be easy having a mom that sent her away because she drinks too much or a dad who took off without even saying good-bye. But that doesn't mean she has to hog all of Jack's time. Or talk his ear off every time she sees him. They even sit together on the bus to school now. I'm always in the seat right behind them, and they don't seem to mind that I'm there, but sometimes they'll put their heads together or talk real low like they don't want me to hear. That's when I get really annoyed. I know Jack saw her first, but I was the one who helped her get to know him. Us, really. Not just him. Both of us. And now they're acting like it's just them.

Like I don't even exist anymore.

Miss Rhodes might be old, but she has a lot of energy. Every morning, she claps her hands and says the same thing, with the same amount of excitement in her voice: "Who's ready to learn more about the Spartans?" All the boys start yelling and waving their *Tito the Warrior* books in the air. They think Tito is the coolest person ever, now that we've learned about all the brave, bloody things he did.

"All right," Miss Rhodes says, smiling broadly this morning. "Where did we leave off yesterday?"

"We were talking about the ways they lined up for battle!" Mitch Stevens yells from the back row.

"Ah, that's right," Miss Rhodes answers. "Who remembers what that was called?"

Multiple hands shoot up in the air.

Miss Rhodes surveys the class, looking pleased. "Jeremy?"

"It was called a flanks formation," Jeremy answers.

"Very close." Miss Rhodes walks over to the board and writes out a word: PHALANX. "It's pronounced 'FA-links,'" she says. "And what does this word mean?"

"It means they stood side by side, locking their shields and moving like one gigantic wall," Jeremy answers. "No one ever broke ranks or fell behind. That way, the enemy never got through."

"Excellent," Miss Rhodes says. "Now let's talk a little bit about the weapons they used. Which, out of all of them, was the most important?"

I'm only listening with one ear, because I already know the answer. Any Spartan warrior's most essential tool in battle was his shield, an enormous bronze disc that weighed close to thirty pounds. Besides protecting them from enemy blows, a hoplite shield was also used as a weapon on its own and to carry the dead off the field.

Instead I'm thinking about what Dad did. Or at least what I think he did. Him and Jack, together. I still can't get those words out of my head. *Spider-Man. Batman. Middlebury.* Or the way Jack's face looked when he saw the Batman mask on the floor of his room. The way he grabbed my wrist and yelled at me to write down what I knew in my little pink book and then told me that everything was going to be okay. Why does everyone say that everything is always going to be okay?

What if it isn't?

What if it never is again?

At least Molly and Susan don't seem to mind that I'm so quiet anymore. They save me a seat every day at lunch and even though they mostly just talk to each other, I don't feel left out. At least, not really.

"Oh my gosh," Susan says today. "I must have worked on my Spartan paper for, like, four hours last night, and I'm still only on the first paragraph! It's gonna take me forever!" She spears a pineapple chunk with the tines of her fork and examines it before popping it in her mouth. Susan does that with all her food, even French fries. She says you never know what might be on them, that one time her little brother was shoveling tater tots in his mouth, and he didn't realize that there was a bug on one of them. He ate the bug, along with the tater tot, and then promptly threw up.

"Why's it taking you so long?" Molly tosses her head. "I'm already halfway through mine. It's not that big a deal."

"It is when you hate to write!" Susan rolls her eyes, chewing. "I'd rather poke my eyes out than write a dumb essay."

"Well, you still have lots of time," Molly says. "It's not even due for three more weeks."

"That's how long I'm going to need just to get through the next *para*graph." Susan looks over at me. "How about you, Pippa? Did you start on your Spartan paper yet?"

I nod, making a little space with my thumb and index finger.

"Just a little?" Susan encourages.

I nod again.

"Do you think it's hard?" she asks.

I nod a third time. I do think it's hard. It's actually one of the hardest things I've ever done in my life. I'd been excited about it earlier, thinking how perfectly Mom fit the mold when it came to being a Spartan warrior, but finding the right words to say it in the kind of way that I want to has been a lot more difficult than I thought.

"Who's your paper about?" Molly asks Susan.

"My great-grandfather," Susan says. "He seriously could've been a real-life Spartan warrior. He was a soldier in World War II, and during one of the battles, he got captured by the Germans. They kept him in a cell for eighteen months and by the time the Americans came in and rescued him, he was covered with rat bites and he only weighed eighty-six pounds."

"Ewwww." Molly shakes her head. "That's disgusting."

Susan scowls.

"I mean about the rat bites," Molly says. "The rest is pretty cool."

Susan glances at me and inspects another piece of pineapple. "He's in a wheelchair and everything now, but when he comes to the presentations, he's going to wear his army uniform. With all his medals." She pops the fruit in her mouth and points at Molly with her fork. "How about yours? Who's it about?"

"My uncle Roy," Molly answers. She sits up a little straighter and shakes her hair. "He got hit by a train when he was a little boy and lost his leg. But now he's the president of this huge plastics company that he built all by himself, and he's a millionaire!" She raises one of her eyebrows. "I bet he'll drive to school in a limo."

"Oh my gosh," Susan says. "That's so cool!" She looks over at me. "How about yours, Pippa? Who's your paper on?"

I shake my head.

"You don't want to say?" Susan asks.

I shake my head again. I don't think I'd want to say even if I could talk. Not now. Not yet.

"Okay." Susan smiles at me. Suddenly, she frowns. "Wait, how're you going to present yours?"

I look down at my tray.

Molly stops chewing. "Yeah, I didn't think of that. We all have to stand up and read our papers, Pippa. Out loud."

I look up again, but only for an instant.

"Do you want me to read yours?" Susan asks.

"Or me?" Molly chimes in. "I'll do it for you, Pippa."

I press my lips together so I don't cry. The weird thing is I don't know where the tears are coming from. Is it because I'm embarrassed? Because I'm grateful? Or is it because deep down I have a terrible feeling that I've made a mistake choosing to write about Mom? She won't be there the way everyone else's person of honor will. And even if I could find all the words in the world to tell everyone how much of a Spartan warrior she was, I don't want those words to come out of someone else's mouth.

They should only be coming out of mine.

Except that they're stuck.

And I still have no idea how to get them out.

Chapter 32
JACK

"Who was able to use the word *guile* in a sentence?" Mr. Lavery, our English teacher, leans back in the wide, black leather chair behind his desk and props his shiny shoes up on one corner. First the right, and then the left, one on top of the other. He does this every day as we settle in, as if he's getting ready to watch a football game.

Various hands go up around the room, including Ben's. He's in his usual spot by the front window with John and Matt. I am on the other side of the room, a few rows behind them.

"Go for it, Ben," says Mr. Lavery.

"I guiled my mother so that she would give me an extra piece of cake." Ben reads his sentence from his notebook, following the words with his index finger. I have to give him credit. For being one of the weakest students in the class, he always gives it a go, even if his answers are almost always wrong.

"Not quite," Mr. Lavery says, steepling his fingers beneath his chin. "*Guile* means what again?"

Ben glances down at his notebook. "Using dishonest methods to achieve a result."

"Correct." Mr. Lavery nods. "And what part of speech is it?"

Ben stares at his paper. "A noun," he says finally.

"Look at your sentence again," Mr. Lavery says. "Have you used the word as a noun?"

Ben is about as weak a grammar student as you can get. I'm no genius when it comes to it either, but I do remember my parts of speech and how to use them. For the most part.

"No?" Ben answers.

"No," Mr. Lavery says. "You've used it in your sentence as a what?"

Ben's eyes begin to shift around the page, as if looking for the answer. That's when John leans forward and whispers something under his breath.

"A verb?" Ben asks.

"Are you asking me, or are you telling me?" Mr. Lavery swings his feet off the desk, hitches his pants up around his waist, and starts meandering around the room.

"I'm telling you," Ben says.

"Good," Mr. Lavery answers. "Shift your sentence around now, so that the word *guile* is being used as a noun."

Ben's forehead begins to furrow, a sure sign that he is completely lost. I know he has just as much chance answering correctly as we do of ever speaking today. Mr. Lavery crosses his arms and waits a few moments. When Ben doesn't answer, he looks around the rest of the room. "Can anyone help Mr. Crenshaw out?"

For a moment the room is silent. I'm pretty sure I know the answer, but I'm not going to say anything. It's kind of an unspoken rule that you don't show another guy up in school. Especially in English class. Even if you're not friends anymore.

Finally, Stella Rutherford, who has one gigantic eyebrow across the middle of her forehead, and is a grammar genius, raises her hand.

"I know Stella knows the answer," Mr. Lavery says, looking at the rest of us. "And I appreciate your willingness to share, Stella, but I'd like to hear from the rest of you, too. Jack, how about you?"

I shake my head, look down at my notebook.

"Oh, I think you might be able to figure it out." Mr. Lavery walks over to my desk and glances at my notebook. "You've used it correctly in your own sentence. Help Mr. Crenshaw out please, Jack. I'll even start you off. 'To get an extra piece of cake . . .'"

I can feel the pressure of Mr. Lavery's presence next to me. He's even got a hand on my shoulder, as if he's going to crush me in my seat if I don't answer. "'I used extreme guile,'" I answer quickly, reading off my paper. My words are barely audible, but Ben turns and shoots daggers in my direction.

"Exactly right," Mr. Lavery says, still perusing my work from where he is standing. "Thank you, Jack. Why don't you share your sentence using the word *contentious* with the class? It's a good one."

I glance down at my notebook. *My father and I have a contentious relationship, which is something I never thought we'd have.* Well, I won't be saying that one out loud. To anyone.

"Jack?" Mr. Lavery taps his red pen against the bottom of his chin. "We're waiting."

"Uh, my sister and I have a contentious relationship because she is very annoying," I say, thinking quickly.

Out of the corner of my eye, I see Ben lean over and mutter something to John, who laughs and nods. Idiots, both of them. They can have each other, for all I care.

"Excellent," Mr. Lavery says, looking slightly puzzled. "Thank you, Jack."

Everyone swarms for the door when the bell rings. I guess I could have been more careful, but I don't really care enough, so when Ben and I collide trying to get out of the classroom, I give him a little bit of a shove which in turn, leads him to give me a big shove, which for some reason, makes me see red.

"Lay off, man," I say, pretending not to notice John

and Matt and Randy circling behind Ben like a pack of hyenas. *This is really it*, I think to myself. *It's really them against me now.*

"You pushed me first." Ben glowers at me, and for the first time ever, I see his height and size as a serious drawback. He really could hurt me if he wanted to. For some reason, the thought of this makes me so angry that my whole face flushes hot.

"I did not," I mutter, pushing past him again. "Don't be such an idiot."

"There's that word again!" Ben yells behind me. "You sound like a parrot, you know that? Can't you come up with something a little more original?"

It takes everything I have not to turn around and barrel headfirst into him, especially since I can hear John, Matt, and Randy laughing too. I walk quickly toward the bathroom, desperate to get away from them before I explode or do anything I'll regret.

Or before any of them see my furious, useless tears.

"Can I ask you something?"

"Sure." Shelby lets another rock sail from her fingers; it skips *onetwothreefourfivesixseveneightnine* times before disappearing beneath the surface. "Dang it! I wanted ten." She turns and plops down next to me. "Sorry. Shoot."

We're sitting on Finster's Rock, where we've been meeting almost every night for the past few weeks. It's hard to believe that we've become such good friends. Especially because of how things started. And because Shelby didn't want any friends to begin with. It's funny how things can change like that. How people can change like that.

"Say we walked back to the house right now, and you saw your dad on the front porch. What would you say?"

Shelby drops the rock she's been fingering and stares out at the lake for a long moment. "You mean what would I *want* to say to him?" she asks. "Or what would I actually say?"

I shrug. "Both, I guess. But start with what you'd want to say."

Her eyes crease at the corners. "I'd *want* to say, 'Where you been?'" She pauses, looking at me out of the corner of her eyes. "Maybe throw in a few unladylike names in there." She picks up a rock and tosses it into the lake. It makes a loud plop. "I'd also *want* to say, 'Why'd you think I'd be okay with you droppin' me like some kind of hot potato? Don't you know I have feelin's? Don't you know what I been goin' through?'" She pauses. "'You *jerk*. You dumb, stupid, selfish *jerk*.'"

I nod. I'd probably want to say something like that to her father, too, if I was in her shoes. Actually, I can hear myself saying exactly that to Dad. More or less. "Okay. What would you actually say?"

Shelby bites her lip. In front of us, the last remnants of the waves from a passing motorboat roll in, flattening at the water's edge and leaving a rim of foamy bubbles.

"I probably wouldn't say anythin'," she says finally. "I'd probably just run to him."

I nod.

I know.

I would, too.

Chapter 33
PIPPA

"Haven't seen you in a while," Nibs says behind me. The dock creaks under her step. She looks like a bear, with an enormous brown afghan around her shoulders and a gray wool hat pulled down low over her ears. Steam rises out of the top of the two mugs she's holding, twirling and disappearing into the air. "Where you been, sweets?"

I point to the house.

"Getting tired of coming out here?" Nibs settles herself next to me, handing me one of the mugs and tightening the afghan under her chin. "Or just getting tired of me?"

I shake my head. I'll never get tired of the dock. And I feel the same way about Nibs. But I haven't wanted to go outside much. Not since I found out about Dad. I've gotten less scared of the police showing up, since it's been a few weeks now and nothing's happened. But I still feel really nervous about Nibs. I guess it's because she was the one who read me that article. I don't think she's put anything together, but you never know. Nibs is a pretty smart lady.

"Here." She opens the afghan, enclosing me in it. I press up against her, holding my mug tightly with both hands. We sit there for a long moment without saying anything. The sweet smell of vanilla drifts up from the mugs, tickling the tip of my nose. On the other side of the lake, the sun is just starting to peek over the rim; pink and white clouds break apart on both sides of it like cotton candy.

What if she knew about Dad? I can't imagine what she'd think if I came into her house one day and showed her the newspaper article. What she would she say if I showed her the Batman or the Spider-Man mask.

"Can you believe it's almost October?" Her voice cuts through my thoughts. She sighs deeply. "Look at all those colors. It's like a patchwork quilt, isn't it?"

I nod, taking a small sip from my mug, then frown. It doesn't taste like it usually does.

Nibs is watching me. "I'm out of blueberry syrup. I had to make you one of mine, with the vanilla and cinnamon. Is it okay?"

I nod and take another sip so she doesn't feel bad. But I don't like it as much as the blueberry.

"How's it going with Miss Rhodes?" Nibs asks.

I shrug.

"Can you tell me in your notebook?" She gives me a little nudge. "Write it down?"

"I'm stuck on my paper," I write.

"The Spartan paper?" Nibs asks.

I nod.

"But I thought you said that was all set. Didn't you tell me . . ." Her voice drifts off as I bend my head again to write. "I thought it was all set," she reads. "But I changed my mind." She nods. "Okay. So you changed your mind. That's hardly the end of the world. You just start again."

"But it's due in two weeks," I write. "And I still can't think of anything."

Nibs is quiet for a moment. Then she says, "Sometimes the best way to find an answer is not to look for it. Do something else. Anything else except the paper. And you watch—one of these days, a new idea will pop right into your head. Right when you least expect it."

I frown and put my pen down. That doesn't sound like very good advice to me. Why would I make myself not think about something I'm supposed to be thinking about?

Nibs squeezes her arm around me. "What else is bothering you?" she asks. "I know it's not just this paper for school."

I get nervous when she does this. It's like she can read my mind or something. Like she can see inside me. Down deep, where all my words are hiding. I shake my head, hoping she'll drop it.

"Does it have anything to do with Jack?" she asks. "Or a certain young girl he seems to have taken a liking to?"

I look over at her, frowning. *She's* noticed that they're leaving me out, too? How embarrassing.

"I don't care about either of them," I scribble quickly.

Nibs pushes her bottom lip out after reading my answer. "Oh, I know," she says. "But let me tell you a story. A long, long time ago, I used to live in a little town called Goose Creek in South Carolina. And then one day, I decided that I needed a new start, and I drove up here. I bought this house, dug myself a garden, and found a teaching job. And"—she pauses here, making eye contact with me—"I met your mother next door. She was just a teenager then, not even fourteen yet. She was a shy little thing too; I barely heard her say a word the whole first year I was here. But I noticed her working in a little garden of her own, right over there, right under Jack's tree house. And she had the biggest, most beautiful tomatoes I had ever seen in my entire life. When I tell you I was jealous of those tomatoes, Pippa . . ." Nibs shakes her head. "My whole *world* went green with envy. I had to find out how she did it. So I went over one day and introduced myself and asked her what her secret was to growing those gorgeous tomatoes. And do you know what your mother told me?"

I shake my head, wide-eyed.

Nibs leans in. "She said she talked to them."

I draw back, confused.

"That's exactly what I did!" Nibs laughs, pointing at me. "I looked at your mother like she was plumb crazy. Talking to plants! Who in their right mind talks to plants?" She turns her head and looks out over the water. "But you know what? It was such a crazy, foolhardy idea that I knew I had to try it. So I did! Every morning that summer when I went out to water my row of tomato plants, I talked to them."

"What did you say?" I write in my book.

"Well, everything and anything, really," Nibs says. "Something like, 'Good morning, gentlemen. I hope you all had a fine rest last evening. I know you're looking forward to all the sunshine coming in today, so stretch out those long arms of yours and get a nice, long suntan. There's no rain forecast for the next three days, so I'm going to water you a little extra so none of you get too thirsty.'"

I smile a little, thinking of Nibs having a one-way conversation with her tomato plants, imagining the tomatoes listening inside their hard, green skins.

"And you know what?" Nibs asks.

I shake my head, although I think I do know what.

"I ended up with the most beautiful, rosy-red, perfectly ripe tomatoes I had ever seen in my entire life." Nibs nods. "I brought them over for your mother to see, and she was so happy for me she laughed out loud. I'd never even seen her smile 'til then. We were friends from that day on, your Mom and me, always talking from our gardens about this and that.

"And then one day, your dad showed up." Nibs nods, as if remembering. "He came to her high school graduation party along with a bunch of other people and stayed until the very end. I remember watching them sit together at the end of this very dock after everyone left. They talked for hours that night. *Hours*. And I knew that things would change a little between us. Not in a bad way necessarily, but in a different way."

"Were you sad?" I write. "Because he took her away from you?"

"No." Nibs shakes her head. "That's the whole point of this story. Your father didn't take her away from me. He just showed your mother that she could open her heart a little bit more. A little bit wider. That she could let us both in." Nibs nods again and this time when I look over at her, I can see something glistening in her eyes.

"We were always friends, Pippa," Nibs says. "Right up to the end."

Up to the end.

Something comes to me suddenly that I haven't thought of before. "Did you ever go see her in the hospital?" I write quickly.

Nibs nods. "Several times. She was always asleep. But I'd sit there and hold her hand and just talk to her. Tell her what was going on down here, how my plants were doing, what the sky looked like that morning. When I'd last seen Mr. Thurber." She looks up, searching the sky, as if he might appear suddenly. "I miss her," she says softly. "I miss her too, Pippa. Every single day."

Chapter 34
JACK

"What if you knew something really bad about someone?" It's my turn for Deep Dark Questions on Finster's Rock. "But if you told anyone about it, that person would get into huge trouble?"

Shelby takes a bite of her Snickers bar and looks out at the lake for a moment. "Depends on who 'someone' is. Is it a person you care about?"

I nod, sliding my hands under my legs so she can't see them trembling.

"Okay, then." She puts the candy bar down next to her and pulls up the thick blue socks she's been wearing since the temperature started dropping. They make her legs look like Popsicle sticks, peeking out from the tops of her pink cowboy boots. "How bad is really bad?"

"*Really* bad."

"Like how bad?"

"Really, really bad."

"Jack!"

I wish I could tell her. I really do. It's not that I want to get Dad in trouble. I'll never do that. But sometimes it feels worse, keeping it all locked up inside. Sometimes I think that as awful as it would be to tell, it would be even worse not to. Like having a cancer inside of you that's eating you alive, and not having any medicine to heal it.

"Is it like hurting someone bad?" Shelby's looking at me worriedly. "Is someone hurting you, Jack?"

"No, nothing like that."

"Is someone else being hurt?"

I shake my head again. "No, no one else either." At least, not on the outside.

I throw a small twig into the water and watch as it floats along the opaque surface. Leaves have started to clutter the edges of the lake, all different colors of them, in every shape and size: small yellow aspen, red maple, and deep orange oak. Before she got sick, Mom used to take Pippa and me for walks around the lake every fall to look for different-colored leaves. We'd get hundreds of them, each one whole and unblemished, and then bring them home where Mom would iron them between sheets of waxed paper. We'd cut them out and poke holes through the top and string them all over the house so that we'd have fall leaves all year round. So that we wouldn't forget how beautiful things were, Mom said, just before they left again.

Shelby snaps her fingers in front of my face. "Hello? Anyone in there?"

I blink and shake my head a little. If only I could do that in real life. Blink, and make it all okay again. Bring things back to the way they were. The way they used to be. "Yeah, I'm here."

"Well, you're goin' to have to talk serious here if you want a serious answer." She picks up the candy bar again and takes another bite. "If no one's hurting you or anyone else, then how bad is really bad?"

I turn my head and stare into her green eyes. There's no use talking about this. I'm not going to be able to say it. Not out loud. Besides, what did she say Nibs told her on the way home from the airport that first day? That there was no point living in the past or the future? That all we had was this moment right now? "You know what? I'm just freaking out. It's nothing, really."

"You sure?"

I nod. I've never been more unsure about anything. But all I have is this moment right now. And it might never come again.

I take a deep breath.

And then I lean over and take her hand in mine. It's warm and softer than anything I ever thought possible. I close my fingers around hers and look up, hoping she doesn't pull away. She's stopped chewing. She's smiling. And then, before I realize what's happened next, she leans over and rests her head on my shoulder.

OCTOBER

Chapter 35
PIPPA

All around the lake, the trees are new colors. Pomegranate red. Pale orange. Lemon yellow and lime green, and even a few patches of dark purple. Vermont is famous for two things: maple syrup and fall. People come from all over just to look at our leaves, to stare at the beautiful colors and take pictures of the sunlight coming through them. But as I sit on the dock this morning, wrapped in Mom's sweater, I can't help thinking that as pretty as autumn is, all the warm months are gone now. Pretty soon, the cold will come, and we'll have months and months of icy, frigid weather. Lake Saint Catherine will freeze over, so thick in some spots that even the ice fisherman won't be able to dig through it for fishing holes. The winter wind will snap and howl, rattling the shutters on the windows and making the house groan, and the snow will come in deep, sugary drifts, blanketing the world around us. Which means that unless Mr. Thurber took off one day without bothering to say good-bye, he doesn't stand a chance of making it to spring.

"All right, everyone." Miss Rhodes claps her hands to get our attention. "Today is Monday, which means that we have just two days left to get everything in order before we give our Spartan presentations on Friday."

"That's three days!" Raymond Dutters calls out, counting off on his fingers. "Tuesday, Wednesday, Thursday."

"You don't have school on Wednesday," Miss Rhodes corrects Raymond. "It's a teacher's in-service day, which means only the teachers need to be here. So we only have *two* days together to get things in order."

"Oh." Raymond sits back in his seat. "No one told me about a teacher's in-service day. Sweet!"

Miss Rhodes gives Raymond a look. She's told everyone about the teacher's in-service day every morning for the last two weeks. Plus, she doesn't like it when students talk without raising their hands first. "All right now," she says, "since we are expecting so many outside guests this year, the presentation itself is going to be moved into Mrs. Paciotti's room."

"You mean the music room?" Raymond calls out again.

"Yes, I mean the music room." Miss Rhodes nods. "And if you keep shouting out, Raymond, you and I are going to have a problem. You know how many times I've asked you to raise your hand first if you have a comment."

"Yes, Miss Rhodes," Raymond mumbles.

Susan raises her hand.

"Yes, Susan?"

"There aren't any seats in the music room," Susan says anxiously. "And my great-grandpa is in a wheelchair. Where will everyone sit?"

I look back and forth between Susan and Miss Rhodes. Susan is right; the only seats in the music room are the elevated steps that have been built into one wall. They're supposed to look like bleachers so that we can practice singing in such a formation for the winter and spring concerts, but I doubt any of the guests will want to sit on them. They're dirty from all of our feet traipsing up and down them all the time, and most of the bottom rows are polka-dotted with wads of old gum.

"The janitors will be bringing in chairs from other rooms," Miss Rhodes says. "Don't worry. Everyone will have a place to sit."

Susan sits back in her seat, but she doesn't look convinced. I don't know what she's so worried about. Not only do I not have a guest coming to the presentation on Friday, I don't even have a presentation! The truth is, after I decided not to do it on Mom, I kind of gave up. I guess I could do it on Dad, but I just don't want to. And that makes me not want to write about anyone else, either.

"We will be bringing in a real podium." Miss Rhodes points to the one at the front of the room, and then walks over to stand behind it. "And just like I do every day, you will all get up, stand behind the podium, and give your speech to the audience."

A murmur of excitement ripples throughout the room. Not only are outside visitors coming in, but we are going to be giving them a show. A real one, behind a podium, with a microphone!

I slump down a little farther into my seat.

"I've also ordered these red sashes." Miss Rhodes holds up a long, crimson colored piece of fabric. It looks like a very large, very wide red belt. Gold lettering has been stitched along the front of it that reads SPARTAN WAR-RIOR. "After your speech, you will go over and put your Spartan sash around your guest, like this." She demonstrates, slipping the sash around her neck and then inserting her left arm through the middle of it until it sits neatly along the front of her chest. "Just like that."

"Awesome!" Raymond shouts out again and the rest of the class agrees, clapping their hands and nodding their heads. Miss Rhodes looks thrilled, too. She doesn't even say anything to Raymond about not raising his hand before making a comment.

"And when everyone is finished, we'll all come back in here for cake and punch," she says. "Your guests can look at your Spartan pictures, your book reports, and anything else you'd like to show them. Now, in a minute,

I'd like everyone to come up to my podium and practice talking for a few minutes. Just to get the feel of it. So it's not so scary for you on Friday."

Molly raises her hand. "Miss Rhodes," she says, "what if someone doesn't want to give their speech on Friday? Like, they're too scared or something, or they get stage fright?"

"That's why we're going to practice now," Miss Rhodes replies. "To avoid that very thing."

"Yeah, but what if it doesn't help?" Molly presses. "What if someone just won't talk anyway?"

Heads turn toward me. Everyone's staring, except Molly, who sits there, blinking innocently at Miss Rhodes.

Miss Rhodes tucks a piece of blonde hair behind one ear. "Are *you* going to have a problem speaking on Friday, Molly?"

"Oh no." Molly shakes her head. "I don't get stage fright."

"Then you have nothing to worry about, do you?"

Molly opens her mouth to reply and then closes it again, like a fish.

But after class, Miss Rhodes asks me to stay. "Is your essay finished, Pippa?" she asks.

I nod.

"Completely finished? And you're happy with it? With the length, the writing, what it says?"

I nod again.

"How about Friday?" Miss Rhodes says. "Have you thought at all about what you'd like to do?"

I stare at the tips of my shoes, chew my bottom lip.

"Would you like me to read your essay for you?" Miss Rhodes' voice is very gentle.

I would not like Miss Rhodes to read my essay for me. But I don't want anyone else reading it either, no matter who it's about, especially Molly or Susan or anyone else in my class. I don't want their help. I know they're curious about me, but I'm starting to think that because I can't give them any answers, they're getting frustrated. Which makes them start to act mean.

"Pippa?"

I nod my head yes.

"You'll let me read it for you?" Miss Rhodes looks relieved, as if a weight has lifted off her back.

I nod again.

What choice do I have?

Chapter 36
JACK

Dad comes into my room again the next morning, while Pippa's out on the dock. "Hey, buddy."

I'm sitting on the edge of my bed, getting dressed for school, although I've just pulled a sock over the one I already have on. I keep doing things like that lately. My brain isn't working right. Yesterday, after my bread popped out of the toaster, I took it out, buttered it, and put it right back in the toaster. I've heard that liking girls can do funny things to you, but I didn't know it went this far. I didn't know it made you loopy.

I look over as Dad sits down on the bed next to me and puts an arm around my shoulders. "How you been?"

"I'm okay." I pull the second sock off the first and put it on my other foot. "What's up?"

"Not much."

"No?"

There's a long pause. "It's all gone." Dad stares at the floor. "We're completely tapped again."

He doesn't have to say anything else. I already know what "it" is and what's coming next. My brain pauses, hits reverse, thinks back again, just to be sure. He hasn't been in my room in weeks. And he only calls me buddy when something serious comes up.

"Already?" I can barely get the words out of my mouth. My hands shake as I try to button my shirt.

"I told you it wouldn't take long." Dad grimaces. "It never does."

"And you can't find a job? Anywhere?"

"The market's terrible right now. It really is. No one's hiring. I still have resumes out all over the place, but I haven't gotten a single call."

"So you're . . ." I swallow. "You're going again?"

Dad nods.

"Where?" I lean over to tie my shoes. My nose is tingling.

"Sandridge." Dad clasps his hands together, studies the floor between his feet. Sandridge is at least an hour and a half west of us. I've never been there, but Ben went last year to a huge farm show where they displayed all kinds of tractors and other equipment. Sandridge isn't as small or ritzy as Middlebury. It probably has bigger banks.

"When?"

"Tomorrow. You don't have school, right? It's a teacher's in-service day?"

"Dad." I stand up from the bed and walk across the room. Place my hands on top of my dresser, as if to steady myself. "Come on. Don't."

"I've got it all scoped out, buddy. There's nothing to worry about. I've gone twice now and looked around. The bank's three times the size as the one in Middlebury, which means I can get in and out of there three times as fast." He takes a deep breath. "But I'm really going to need your help this time. There are a lot more tellers than the one in Middlebury. You're going to have to distract them so they don't notice me."

I bite my lip so hard I can taste blood.

"We'll get at least three times the amount of money we got last time," Dad says.

"*You* got last time." I spin around, raging suddenly. "*You* robbed the bank in Middlebury, Dad. Not me."

His head drops, as if absorbing the blow of my words. Then he raises it again. Looks steadily at me.

"Pippa knows," I say quickly, although I'd already promised myself I wouldn't tell him. "And not just because of the articles in the paper. She found the masks, Dad. Both of them."

"What are you talking about?" His face pales.

"She found the Spider-Man one on the floor of the living room the night we drove to Middlebury." Dad's eyes dance across the floor, as if connecting puzzle pieces.

236

"And then she went rooting around in your car and found the Batman one. And the pillowcase. She figured it all out."

He sits down heavily on the bed. "And?"

"And what?"

"And . . . what did she say? What did you say? To her?"

"I didn't say anything to her." I turn back around, stare at my reflection in the oval mirror above my dresser. There are dark shadows under my eyes, a red pimple on my chin. My hair is clean, but the front of it hangs in my eyes, the bottom of it down to my shoulders. I look different, I think suddenly. Older. When did that happen?

"You didn't tell her anything?" Dad repeats.

"No. Nothing. I told her that whatever she was thinking she was wrong and to forget about it." I turn back around. "But I know she knows, Dad. She's not a dumb little girl."

"She never was." Dad stands up from the bed. "Which means we're not going to try to hide it from her anymore."

My heart skips. "What's that supposed to mean?"

"I'll talk to her." Dad nods. "Don't worry. I'll take care of it."

Chapter 37
PIPPA

"My mom and I went up to the mall last night and I got the most beautiful dress for Friday," Molly says at lunch. "It's green with little white buttons down the back and this big poufy skirt. And my mom even let me get shoes to match. With heels!"

"Heels?" Susan looks away from the sliced carrot she's inspecting and raises an eyebrow. "How high?"

"Oh, you know." Molly shrugs. "Just little tiny ones."

Susan glances in my direction. I know she's anxious about things between Molly and me. The three of us have been friends for so long that even I can't imagine anything different. But I haven't even looked at Molly since she asked Miss Rhodes the question about someone not speaking at the presentations. I know she was talking about me. And she knows I know, which is probably why she hasn't looked at me either. Last night, when

I was lying in bed thinking about it, I decided that I might be okay with losing Molly as a friend. She's always been pretty loud, and one time I heard her say something really rude about how fat Jenna Lafferty had gotten. But I don't want to lose Susan, too. I like Susan. She's much quieter than Molly. And except for that dumb thing she said on the first day about me needing time (which wasn't actually so dumb at all) she's always been nice to me. Always.

"How about you, Pippa?" Susan asks now. "You going to wear anything special on Friday?"

I shrug and fiddle with my peas. The truth is, what I'm going to wear is the absolute last thing on my mind. I have less than forty-eight hours to finish a paper I haven't even started, and I don't even know who I'm going to write it on. Maybe I'll just make someone up. An Uncle Felix or some other imaginary relative who survived the sinking of the *Titanic* as a little kid and then grew up to be an Olympic swimmer. I'll have both his parents die on the *Titanic*, maybe even create a scene where he drifted for a while, hanging only to a chunk of life raft in the middle of the ocean, before he was finally rescued. Actually, that's perfect. Why didn't I think of something like this before?

"You have to wear something nice," Molly says, jerking me from my thoughts. "I mean, it's a *formal* presentation, Pippa. Lots of people are coming."

I shrug again, not because I don't care, but because I suddenly feel lighter. Better. Like maybe Friday won't be such a catastrophe after all. Even if the whole thing is a lie.

But Molly narrows her eyebrows. "Is that all you can do?" She lifts her shoulders dramatically and then lets them drop. "Shrug? You look like a monkey, you know that? Shrug, shrug, shrug."

"Molly!" Susan gasps, watching me. Her eyes are huge, and her tiny hands are gripping the edge of the table.

"Don't you get it?" Molly is glaring at me. "All this 'I can't talk' routine is just an act so she doesn't have to do as much work as the rest of us."

"Molly, stop it." Susan looks at her. "You're just being mean."

"No, I'm not." Molly stands up, holding her tray in front of her. "I'm just saying out loud what everyone else in this school is thinking. Including you, Susan." And with a swish of her hair, she turns around, and stalks off.

I look over at Susan. She's watching Molly move across the cafeteria, the curtain of her long, blonde hair swishing across the middle of her back. I wonder if she's thinking what I'm thinking: that I'll probably never talk to Molly again. That maybe such a thing will not be the end of the world.

Then Susan looks over at me. Her cheeks are pink. "I've never thought that, Pippa," she says. "Not once."

I believe her. And I'm glad that Molly's not there when I slide my hand over and place it on top of hers. Molly would have rolled her eyes at such a thing. Susan, though, smiles and covers my hand with her own.

Chapter 38
JACK

"What's the matter?" Shelby asks for the fifth time as the bus hurtles toward school. She's all bundled up in the red scarf and army-green overcoat she's been wearing for the last two weeks, since the temperature dropped below fifty. "I can't believe you don't think it's freezin'," she said the first day she showed up in it. "I can barely feel my feet."

Pippa and I looked at each other and grinned. "You think it's freezing now?" I shook my head. "Wait until January. This is nothing."

That's what I tell her now when she asks me what's wrong: nothing.

After Dad left my room this morning, I just sort of sat on my bed and felt nothing, too. All the panic and crazy heartbeating just sort of leaked out of me as he walked out and shut the door, as if another door, deep inside my chest, had closed too. A terrible silence filled the room and everything was very still, and for a whole moment, it felt as if I was suspended in space, or had settled somehow down to the very deepest part of the ocean. It was like watching myself in a dream—and not being able to do anything about it.

I thought about that moment outside Friendly's. Had that decision led to this one? And if it had, what would come next? How bad would things actually get?

The moment passed, of course, and now I'm back in full-panic mode. But no one needs to know that.

Shelby tickles my cheek with the fuzzy fronds of her scarf. "Come on, I know it's something." Her breath is soft against my cheek. She smells like strawberry Pop-Tarts. "You'll feel better if you tell me."

"No, I won't."

And it's true. I won't. This isn't like the talks we've had at lunch, or even like the ones we've been having on Finster's Rock, where saying things out loud have helped break down some of the walls between us. This one doesn't even involve a wall. It's like being stuck inside a whole fortress. And there's no way out. I can't tell anyone about any of it, because if I do, Dad will get thrown in jail. And for as wrong as I know what he's doing is, I'm not going to be the one to send him to jail.

"I bet you wi-ll." Shelby's using that singsong voice she sometimes uses when she's trying to be funny. She says "wheel" instead of "will," which usually makes me laugh too, but right now, it just makes me feel annoyed.

"Stop, okay?" I push her hand away. Move my head closer to the window. I can feel her tense up, hear her biting her fingernails.

Pippa's reflection turns in the window behind me. She catches my eyes and gives me a smile.

I don't smile back.

———

I have gym last period, and since it's getting pretty cold out, Mr. Michaels lets us play a game of team dodgeball inside.

Team dodgeball is like regular dodgeball, except that there are two teams, and each player gets a chance to take someone on the opposite team out. I bend down and pretend to tie my laces as Ben, who's one of the captains, picks John, Randy, and Matt, and then Sam, Owen, and Jimmy. I'm the last one, standing there like an idiot with all the girls, and I give Ben a look as I jog over to the other side and line up. But I don't care. I really don't. This stuff is a joke compared to what I've got to worry about.

Ben takes out two of our players right off the bat, nailing them in the ankles. He was always good at dodgeball, maybe even the best in our class. He's got a killer left arm, and his aim, even from a distance, is ridiculously accurate.

244

But I'm good, too. And I can tell he's getting frustrated as I peg three of his guys, one right after the other. He starts doing the thing with his shirt, sliding his fists up under it and then punching the material—one, two—as if what he'd really like to do is punch someone's face. He yells as he misses Gary Jenkins by an eighth of an inch, and then he starts hopping up and down. Now I know he's really agitated. When Ben starts hopping up and down, there's no turning back. He's out for blood.

Pretty soon, it's down to five of us—Ben, John, and Matt against Gary and me. Everyone else is on the bleachers, yelling and screaming. I fake a throw to the right and surprise John out of nowhere, smacking the ball against his knee and knocking him to the floor. The class screams. Ben jogs over and yanks John up, making a big show out of patting him on the back, pulling him in close, and saying something in his ear. Then he takes the ball. Nails Gary so hard against the hip that I can hear the intake of air as he gasps.

Mr. Michaels steps in, blowing his whistle. "I appreciate the sense of competition here, gentlemen," he says, "but let's keep it clean." He points at Ben. "Too close, Ben."

Now it's just me against Ben and Matt. It's my ball. I line up as if getting ready to hit Ben. Then I do another fake out and send Matt's feet flying out from under him. Another scream from the bleachers. Matt limps off, shaking his head. Ben and I eye each other across the glossy expanse of floor.

It's his ball. There's no way I'm going to let him get me. Not after what he said at the fishing hole. Not after ignoring me for the last four weeks except to rub it in my face that he's with a new group of friends. Not after not picking me to be on his—

Smack!

The ball whistles through the air. I jump right, anticipating Ben's famous left-hand drive, but it's a mistake. The ball is flying to the right and I jump too soon— directly into its path. It hits me squarely on the knee, and I crash to the floor.

For ten seconds, I don't see anything. Just black, maybe a few pinpoints of something sparkly around the edges. A sharp, electric-like pain comes from under my chin, but it fades again as I shake my head. Out of the corner of one eye, I can see Mr. Michaels running toward me, across the gym. I turn my head until out of the corner of my other eye, I can see Ben standing there, fists in the air. And before I know what I'm doing, I'm on my feet, rushing toward him.

I charge like a bull, shoulders first, head down. I don't know if he sees me coming, but I know he feels it. Seconds later, after we've stopped sliding across the floor and gotten our bearings, the pummeling starts.

I swing wildly, blindly, grunting as my fists come into contact with his shoulders, his back, his neck. I feel a sharp pain along the side of my eye as Ben gets a few in too, and then suddenly, Mr. Michaels is pulling me off him and holding my arms down tight along my sides, yelling at me to stop.

And just like that, it's over.

Chapter 39
PIPPA

I sit in my regular spot on the bus after school, waiting for Jack and Shelby. They're late today. Real late. In fact, they're still not there when the bus driver shuts the doors and starts moving. I look around anxiously, peering through the windows, but I don't see either of them. Where could they be? Why aren't they here?

Just as the bus starts rounding the corner, a sharp banging sounds near the front. The driver slams on the brakes and flings open the doors.

"Sorry!" Shelby says breathlessly. "I got held up. Thanks for stopping."

"You're lucky I didn't run you over," the driver growls. "Get in."

Shelby scans the bus quickly before heading down the aisle toward me. Her face is pinched with worry and she's biting her nails. "You hear about Jack?" she asks, sliding into my seat.

I clutch her arm, shake my head.

"He got in a fight. During gym. Him and that Ben kid. I wasn't there, but I heard about it. Everyone's sayin' it got pretty wild. Mr. Michaels took him to Principal Moseley's office. Your dad's on his way down, I guess. Big meetin'."

I stare at Shelby, trying to make sense of what she's just said. Jack? A *fight*? I've never known Jack to hit anyone in his life, not even me. *I'm* the one who slugs people—well, him, mostly—when I get mad enough. Jack's never raised his hand to anyone. I take out my pink notebook.

"Is he in trouble?"

Shelby nods, taking her nails out of her mouth. "I think so."

"What's going to happen?"

"Depends on the school rules, I guess. We had a kid down in Texas who brought a slingshot to school and only got a detention. But you know, this is Vermont. Things could be different here."

I bend my head, write again. "Was Ben hurt?"

"Someone said his nose was bleedin'. But that's all."

"Was Jack?"

Shelby shakes her head. "He was holdin' a paper towel or somethin' along the bottom of his chin, but I couldn't tell if it was bleedin' or not."

"You saw him?"

She nods. "Right when they were bringin' him into Principal Moseley's office." She looks down at her hands. "I waved, but he didn't see me."

249

I stare down at my little pink notebook, trying to imagine Jack being led into the principal's office after a fight. His shirt was probably wrinkled, his hair all messed up. He would have been clenching his fists, looking at the floor, embarrassed, angry . . . "Did he look sad?" I write.

Shelby reads the question and looks up at me. "Did he look sad?" she repeats slowly. "Yeah Pippa, you know what? I would've said mad, but I think you're right. I think he did look sad."

———————————

There's a note on the kitchen counter from Dad:

Pip,
  Had to go over to the school to see about Jack.
Nibs will be home in ten minutes. Stay with her until
  we get home. She knows.
  Love,
  Dad

I take a banana out of the bowl in the middle of the kitchen table. Then I head upstairs. I sit in the middle of Jack's bed, unpeel the banana, and eat the whole thing, one bite after the other. Then I lay down. I pull Jack's covers over the top of me and close my eyes. His bed smells like dirty socks and the spicy deodorant he's been wearing ever since Shelby got here. Gross. I throw the covers off again, stare up at a crack in the ceiling.

Once, a really long time ago, while Mom was reading *Charlotte's Web* to Jack in bed, I crept in and slid under the covers. Jack tried to make me leave. He didn't want me to go on Wilbur's journey with them, whatever that meant. He said I was annoying, and that I would just get in the way. But Mom shook her head and gave both of us a kiss. She said that we needed to remember that we were the most important people in each other's lives. And that having the right people with you—on any kind of journey—was everything. Even if we could sometimes be a little annoying. I burrowed down real tight under the blankets next to Jack, with just my head poking out at the top, and stared up at the same crack in the ceiling as Mom read. I didn't have any idea what was going on— there was a pig and a mouse and some goose that stuttered when she talked—but it didn't matter. I remember feeling safe, warm, and completely happy.

I close my eyes against the sting of tears and roll over, pressing my face into the pillow. Maybe those kinds of moments only exist when you're little, because you don't know any better. Because you were just a stupid little kid who thought that nothing bad would ever happen. That nothing bad *could* ever happen because you were tucked inside a sea of blankets next to your big brother, listening to your mother's voice in the dark.

I slide my hands under Jack's pillow, bunching it up to get more comfortable. But my fingers touch something soft. Silky. I pull out the Batman mask. And then the

Spider-Man one. Inside the Batman mask is the neatly folded article about the bank robbery in Middlebury. Inside the Spider-Man mask is the other article that I found with the fish story on the back. I stare at both of them for a long time.

Red and black and blue.

Pig and mouse and goose.

Jack and Dad and me.

Chapter 40
JACK

Once, a few years back, when Dad and I went to pick up
Ben to go play basketball, it started to rain. After a few
minutes, Dad had to pull the car over because it was rain-
ing so hard that you couldn't see anything. Sheets of water
were just pouring down, like we were inside a car wash.
Finally, it stopped and Dad started the car, and we headed
back down the road. But after about two minutes, he had
to stop a second time because a huge tree had fallen across
a telephone pole. "Cool!" Ben and I shouted, dashing out
of the car to inspect the damage. "Hold on!" Dad shouted.
"Don't go any farther!" He was right to be alarmed.
Because not only was the road blocked, but the electrical
wires from the telephone pole were alive, snaking across
the road like bullwhips. Little white sparks shot out of the
bottom every time one of them snapped against the pavement, and the air, still heavy and wet, smelled burnt.

If I ever get around to talking to Ben again, that's
what I would tell him I felt like when I saw him standing

there with his fists in the air—as if one of the wires inside me just sort of snapped. I felt burnt and electric and maybe even a little bit dangerous, too.

———————

"I'd like to hear from you first, Ben," Principal Moseley says. "Why don't you tell us what happened?"

We're all at a big conference table, Dad and me on one side, Ben's mom and him on the other. Mrs. Crenshaw, who has always been nice to me, looks at me now with the same pitiful expression she had at the funeral. I look away quickly, pretend that I haven't seen it. Principal Moseley, who has frizzy brown hair and glasses with bright red frames, is sitting at the end of the table, right in front of the window, and Mr. Michaels is on the other end, opposite her.

Ben shifts in his chair. Lowers the ice pack from his nose. "Like I said, he pushed me to the floor and we got into it."

"Who pushed you to the floor?"

I stare at Principal Moseley as she pushes her glasses up along her nose. She is not a dumb person. Mr. Evans even told us she went to Harvard. So why is she asking such stupid questions?

"He did." Ben points at me without looking in my direction.

"Jack did," Principal Moseley says.

Ben nods.

"Why did he push you?" she asks.

"I don't know." Ben shrugs, raises the ice pack again to his nose. "We won the game and the next thing I know, I'm on the floor."

"The volleyball game?" Principal Moseley asks.

Ben lifts his eyes. And I can tell, as he looks at her, that he's wondering about that Harvard education, too. "Dodgeball," he says quietly.

"Dodgeball." Principal Moseley folds her hands. Looks over at me. "Would you agree with that version of events, Mr. Kendall?"

"Yeah."

Dad pokes me in the ribs.

"Yes, ma'am," I correct myself.

"Anything else you would like to add?" she asks.

I shake my head, feel something swishing around behind my right eye. The skin under it is hot, and when I reach up to touch it with my fingertips, it feels puffy.

"Would you like some ice for that eye?" she asks.

"I'm fine, thanks."

"How about the cut on your chin?"

I lower the paper towel, stare down at the red ink blot in the middle. "It's not bleeding anymore," I answer. "I'm okay."

I stare out the window behind Principal Moseley's head as she launches into a whole speech about safety and respect and physical boundaries. The late afternoon light looks like liquid gold, the way it sometimes does on the lake on very bright sunny days. The leaves on a tree to her right are orange; the one to her left, a deep red, almost cherry color. Somewhere in the distance, I hear the words *three days* and *mandatory in-school suspension.*

"That's kind of a lot, don't you think?" It takes me a moment to realize that the question has come from Ben's mouth. "I mean, I *was* kind of rubbing it in. After I won and everything." He sneaks a glance in my direction but doesn't meet my eyes. "I probably would've freaked a little, too."

Ben's mom puts a hand on his arm. I wonder if Ben's told her anything about us. If she wonders why I haven't been over in so long.

"I appreciate what you're saying," Principal Moseley says. "But acting in an antagonistic manner is one thing. Striking someone is another thing entirely. That kind of behavior will not be tolerated."

"I know," Ben says. "But I'm just saying. I got it in the nose; he got it in the eye. And you know, what's fair is fair."

"Mr. Michaels?" Principal Moseley looks over at our gym teacher. "What do you think?"

"I think a one-day suspension is enough," Mr. Michaels says. "Like Ben said. They both got into it."

"All right." Principal Moseley unfolds her hands and runs them lightly over the surface of the table. "I'm fine with that, then. One day in-school suspension for fighting, Mr. Kendall. But if there's another incident, it will mean serious trouble."

After we all get up, Mrs. Crenshaw shakes Dad's hand and smiles sadly at him. The look on her face says everything she's not saying out loud: *You're a mess without your wife. Your family is going down the tubes. It's such a shame. I'm so sorry. Everything is such a shame.* I glance over at Ben as she drapes his coat over his shoulders, hoping he'll look my way just for a second. *Thanks,* I'd say with my eyes if he did. *I owe you one.*

But he turns around, and with his eyes glued to the floor, walks out of the room.

———————————

Later, much later, after Dad and Pippa and I have eaten dinner and the dishes have been done and we're all sitting in the living room watching TV, there is a knock on the door. Pippa goes to answer it. A few seconds later, she reappears and points at me.

"Who is it?" I ask, although I think I already know.

Pippa puts a hand on her hip and cocks her head. She knows I know.

"Ooooh," Shelby says a few minutes later, looking at my eye. "I didn't know you got hit that hard. Does it hurt?"

"No, it's fine. I've had ice on it since I got home. It looks worse than it is."

"All boys say that." She smiles.

I shrug, look down at my feet.

"How 'bout your chin?"

I lift my head a little, touch the congealed bump along the bottom of it. "It's all right. Might leave a scar, but that's okay."

"Could be a story scar," she says. "The best kind."

"A what?"

"A story scar," she says. "Come on out to Finster's Rock with me and I'll tell you about them. Can you?"

I shake my head no, which isn't true. Dad hasn't said anything about me not going anywhere tonight. But I don't feel like riding to Finster's Rock and rehashing everything that just happened. This was between Ben and me. And I sort of want to keep it that way.

"We don't have to talk about the fight," Shelby says. "We don't have to talk at all, if you don't want."

Actually, that sounds perfect. Except that I can't take perfect right now, either. Everything else is so crazy that it would probably mess up perfect, too. "I'm good. I'm just going to chill here tonight, okay?"

Her face falls.

I pretend not to notice.

"All right, then," she says, giving me a little wave. "I guess I'll see you."

I start to close the door. "Wait."

She turns, eyes wide.

"You didn't tell me what a story scar was."

She smiles. "Ask Pippa. She'll tell you. 'Night, Jack."

I watch her go, pink cowboy boots crunching the gravel along the driveway, the back of her white shirt whipping in the wind. She pulls her coat tighter as she disappears behind Nibs' house and tucks her scarf around one ear.

" 'Night, Shelby," I whisper, shutting the door.

Chapter 41
PIPPA

Dad comes into my room and shakes me awake. "Hi, sweetheart." His breath smells like toothpaste and he's clean-shaven. As I reach up to touch his soft skin with my fingers, he sits down and takes my hand in his. "Jack and I have to head out for the day. We're going up to Sandridge. I've already talked to Nibs, and since you don't have school, she . . ."

But I'm not listening. The alarm is going off in my head. And this time it's loud. Really loud. I sit up. Pull my hand out of his. Shake my head no, over and over again.

"Pip." Dad holds me by the shoulders. "Honey. Listen to me. Jack told me you know what happened in Middlebury. That you found the masks." I raise my eyes, look into his, and try not to cry. He pulls me in for a hug. "It's okay." His voice is muffled because my ear is pressed against his shirt, but I can hear him talking about things like losing Mom's house and the family and how we don't have to worry because . . .

I pull out of his hug and reach for my notebook and pink glitter pen. I write very, very fast inside and then show it to Dad. He shakes his head. "You can't go with us, Pip. You just can't."

I lower my head, write again. My hand is shaking when I turn it out to show him.

"Then I'll tell."

A muscle jumps in his cheek. He stares at me with a bewildered expression on his face and in that moment, my heart breaks into a million tiny pieces.

"Okay," he says finally. "But you can't come into the bank. You have to stay in the car. The whole time. No matter what."

I nod.

"We're leaving in one hour," Dad says. "Get dressed and brush your teeth."

I nod again and close the book.

Then I wrap my arms around his big shoulders and hold on tight.

Jack turns when he hears me on the dock behind him. The black-and-blue streak under his right eye is even bigger than it was last night, and his face looks so sad that when I sit down next to him, I slip my fingers around one of his belt loops and lean in.

"Hey there," he says softly. "What're you dressed for already? You're just hanging with Nibs today."

I look up at him. Shake my head.

His eyebrows narrow. "Yeah. Didn't Dad tell you?"

I take my notebook out. Jack looks over my shoulder, reading the words silently as I write them. "You can't come with us!" He rears back a little, shaking his head. "No, Pippa, you can't."

I bend my head again and write. "I'll stay in the car."

"No. No way. I don't care if you're . . ." His voice drifts off as I start writing again.

Jack reads, his eyes getting big. "You told him you'd tell?" The edges of his nostrils are white. He looks as angry as I've ever seen him. "You'd *do* that?"

I stare back down at my words. They look terrible, suddenly. Wrong. A betrayal of the worst kind. The complete opposite of anything a Spartan soldier would do. I shake my head as the words blur beneath me. A tear falls on the page and then another. I'm scared. I'm so confused.

"Pippa," Jack starts, putting a hand on my shoulder. "Listen to me . . ."

But I shrug him off and turn to a clean page to write something else. Then I turn the book around for Jack to see.

He reads what I've written. Lifts his eyes. For a moment, we just look at one another, as if we're seeing each other for the very first time. As if we might not ever see each other again.

A strange noise sounds behind us. I blink as it comes again, louder this time. It sounds like a frog snoring or the faint pitter-patter of stones thrown against the water.

"Pippa." Jack says my name in a whisper. "Look."

I already know it's Mr. Thurber. But seeing him again, standing there in the middle of the dock with his long, yellow beak and silky feathers feels magical. Almost like seeing Mom again. I feel dizzy, as if someone has blown helium into my head, and I reach out with three fingers to steady myself.

Mr. Thurber is getting ready to say good-bye. He does his usual preening, examining the snow-white feathers along his belly with his beak the way he always does, in preparation for the long flight ahead. His wings open wide, the tipped feathers fluttering along the edges, and he flaps once, twice, a third time. As he tips his long neck back, another burble comes out of his throat, followed by two shorter ones, and then he straightens his head. For a long moment, he just gazes at us with his liquid black eyes, taking us in, putting us somewhere where he won't forget us in the long months ahead. And then, after another moment, he lifts himself into the air. Jack and I sit there for what feels like forever, watching as he rises higher and higher into the sky. Jack takes my hand as the heron moves toward a cloud on the other side of the lake and squeezes as he disappears behind it.

It will be a long time before we see him again. Months and months of cold and ice and snow and sleet.

But then it will get warm. The lake will start to thaw and the snow will melt and the day will come when we catch sight of him cresting around the bend, this time to say hello there, and I've missed you, and how have you been?

Chapter 42
JACK

"That eye looks terrible." Dad reaches out across the front seat with his free hand, but I duck my head. He drops it again, watching me. "It's still pretty swollen, Jack. Does it hurt?"

"Could you just watch the road?" I don't mean for it to come out as rudely as it does. Or maybe I do. Pippa jumps a little in the backseat, and Dad grimaces as he turns his head, settling his gaze on the car in front of us. "My eye is fine." I lower my voice. "I had ice on it all night. It looks a lot worse than it feels."

You'd think he'd gotten his fill of talking about it yesterday on the ride back from school, when he went on and on about how fighting wasn't the answer. "I know what it's like to have things build and build like that," he'd said, tapping his chest with two fingers. "In here. Inside. Until you feel like something's going to blow. The trick is not to let it get that big, Jack. You'll be a lot better off if you can tell someone what's bothering you instead of letting is grow into something unmanageable like that. Trust me. Fighting is never the answer. Never."

"Oh, but robbing banks is?" I shot back.

Dad gritted his teeth, turned his head.

"And who am I supposed to tell, Dad, huh? Who am I supposed to go and confide in that my dad has turned into a bank robber?" I kicked the underside of the car. "How am I supposed to manage *that*?"

"All right," Dad said sharply. "That's enough." He ran a hand through his hair. "Fine, I guess that's fair. You want to take your anger out on me, go ahead. I deserve it. But don't take it out on your friends. You're going to need your friends, Jack. And they'll need you. Don't ruin that."

Now, I close both of my eyes and lean back against the seat. I didn't sleep well, and I'm exhausted. The swelling around my eye has gone down a lot, but it still hurts, and a bunch of other parts on my body ache just enough for me to notice. Including my chin.

"Hey, Pip." I turn around, remembering something. "What's a story scar?"

I wait as she writes in her notebook and then hands it over the seat.

"It's a scar that has a great story about how you got it. Like my knee."

I read her explanation aloud and then give her a look. "Like your knee? What great story is behind the cut on your knee?" I wait as she writes, imagining all the awful scenarios she's creating about me abandoning her that day, or finding out about Dad's empty car lot.

"Meeting Shelby," she writes. "Getting to be her friend."

I give the book back to her slowly. It's not often that Pippa surprises me. But it always feels good when she does.

"I have a story scar," Dad says suddenly. "You want to hear about it?"

Pippa nods her head in the backseat while I rearrange myself again in the front and stare out the window.

Dad's feeling around on the back of his head, fingering pieces of his hair until he stops suddenly and says, "There. Can you see it? Right where my fingers are."

Pippa leans forward, examining his scalp up close, but I don't move. She touches the spot with her finger and then nods, sitting back down.

"I got that scar the very first time I kissed your mother."

I turn my head a quarter of an inch.

"We'd all just graduated from high school, and Grandma and Grandpa Hession threw her a party at the house," Dad continues. "I showed up, totally out of the blue. No invitation, no phone call. No nothing. I wasn't even sure if your mother knew my name. But I'd been so crazy about her for so long by then that I knew if I didn't say something to her that night, the last night we were all going to have an excuse to be together, I'd regret it for the rest of my life."

I don't have to turn around to know that Pippa is watching Dad with her big eyes and drinking in every word. Neither of us have heard this story before.

"I went in and said hello," Dad goes on. "She seemed surprised to see me, but she was perfectly polite. She even went and got me an orange soda from the kitchen when I asked her for a drink. But you know, it was her party. Her night. So I just sort of stood in the corner for a while, watching as she moved around the room and talked with everyone. She was shy, so it was hard for her to do, but she did it. She talked to every single person in the room. Except me. And eventually, I realized that I'd acted like a big idiot, just showing up to this party without an invitation and then just standing there, staring at this beautiful girl who didn't even know my name, and so I got up to go. I was halfway out the door when I heard her voice. 'Sam!' she said. 'Sam Kendall! Where are you going?' I turned around so fast that I cracked my head on the side of the door. Just split it right open. There was blood running down the back of my neck, ruining the good white shirt I'd put on to try to look nice and smearing the floor in big drops. Everyone started rushing around for ice and towels and yelling about the blood, but I didn't notice a thing. Because the only thing I could see was your mother. And the only thing I could hear was her voice, saying my name. Sam Kendall. It was the sweetest sound I'd ever heard in my life."

Dad nods, staring straight ahead. He's a million miles away. So am I.

No one says anything for a moment. Then I hear the sound of scribbling in the backseat. Pippa shoves her book forward. "When did you kiss her?" I read aloud before rolling my eyes. But the truth is that I want to know, too.

"Later that night," Dad says. "After I got all cleaned up, we started talking. And after we started, it was like we couldn't stop, as if all the things we'd wanted to say to each other over the last year or so just came pouring out. Turns out she'd wanted to get to know me, too, but she didn't know how. We were still talking by the time everyone left, and Grandma and Grandpa went upstairs to bed, so we went and sat on the dock and talked some more. We talked the whole night. The whole entire night. It was like a blink of an eye, it went so fast. And then, just as the sun was coming up, I leaned over and kissed her. It was our first kiss. And it all came about because I whacked my head on the side of her door when she said my name." He glances at Pippa in the rearview mirror and then over at me. "So what do you think? Is that a story scar, or what?"

Pippa nods her head vigorously.

But I turn and look out the window again.

He doesn't need to know that I think it's probably the best story scar I'll ever hear. That it's not just his story anymore. It's our family's story. One that I wish could make me proud to be a part of.

But we're on our way to rob a bank.

Which, story scar or not, makes us a family of criminals.

Chapter 43
PIPPA

Sandridge is ugly. Everything is the same boring tan color, even the sidewalks. There are no flowers. No trees. All the buildings are the same size and shape, and they're all brown. So I don't even realize it when Dad pulls the car into the bank parking lot and turns off the engine. But then my heart starts to pound. We're here? Already? I look out the window at the building behind us again. There, in big black letters, are the words SANDRIDGE COMMUNITY BANK.

I turn back around, stare at the back of Jack's head. What is he thinking? Is it about what I wrote in my notebook? And why won't he look at me? Why won't he talk?

Dad gets out of the car and slams the door. He opens the trunk and starts fiddling around. I can hear the sound of things being tossed aside—*thunk, plop*— and I know he's almost done. I jab Jack hard in the shoulder.

"Don't." He doesn't turn around. His voice is hard and clipped, like ice. Despite myself, I do it again, not for him, but for me. I just want to know. I just want to hear.

He whirls around on the second jab and grabs my finger. "I said knock it *off*." His eyes are steely blue, almost gray. I hardly recognize them. I feel scared, like I might cry.

Dad opens the door and tosses in the pillowcase. Jack glances at it and releases my finger. Dad slides inside the car. "All right, buddy," he says. "Let's talk about this."

I sit back against my seat and stare at the side of Jack's face. I feel like I'm going to throw up.

"We don't need to talk about it," Jack says. "I'm not going in. I'm not helping you."

Dad stares at Jack for a minute. He rolls his lower lip over his teeth and then runs a hand through his hair. "This is it," he says. "I promise. After this one, it'll never happen again." He raises a hand. "I swear on your mother."

Jack looks at him. Even from where I'm sitting, I can see something soften in his face. Is it because it will be the last time? Or because Dad just made a promise that he can never, ever take back? *Please Jack, don't. Please. Remember what I wrote.* I'm gripping the edge of the seat so hard I can hardly feel my fingers. *Look at me, Jack. We can be a phalanx, you and I. We'll link arms, move in tight together so that nothing can get through.*

For some reason, he turns. I give him the tiniest shake of my head, hope that he can read the words behind my eyes: *Remember what I wrote. Remember what I said.*

"No," he says, turning his head again. "Middlebury was the last one, Dad. This one isn't going to happen. I'm not going in."

I hold my breath and try not to cry.

Dad inhales sharply through his nose and then lets it out. "I don't have a choice, buddy, okay? I've already gone over everything with you. I'm in the exact same spot that I was when we drove up to Middlebury. This time I'll make sure to get enough money so that I'll have time to find a job. I'm telling you, this is it. No more after this, okay? I promise. But I can't do this one without you. The bank's too big."

"Then don't do it." Jack's voice is flat. "Let's go home."

"I can't. I've got to do it." Dad starts rummaging through the pillowcase. He takes out another mask— Hulk—and shoves it into the front pocket of his jeans.

"Dad." Jack grabs his arm. "Come on. Let's just go home."

"I won't be long." Dad reaches out, grabs the back of Jack's head, and kisses him hard on the forehead. "Sit tight with your sister."

Before I can blink again, he's walking so fast across the parking lot that it almost looks like he's running. I

(right margin, vertical text) PIPPA

grab Jack's arm and shake it. But he's already moving. I watch from the back window as he runs after Dad and grabs him around the arm. Dad whirls around, holding Jack by both shoulders. He's shaking his head, moving his lips, trying to pull Jack back to the car. Jack won't let himself cry as he resists and drags his feet. But he's not strong enough. Dad pushes him back inside, holding him down again with both hands. "Enough, Jack!" His voice is terrible. "That's *enough*!" I wait, but Jack doesn't fight it. He just stares at Dad like he's confused. Like he doesn't know anything anymore.

Dad slams the car door and starts across the parking lot again. The Hulk mask peeks out from his left pocket. The pillowcase swings from his right hand. In the front, Jack begins to tear up. The phalanx formation is broken. But I still have my shield.

I push open the car door and slide out. The sun is right above me, huge and hot and yellow. I open my mouth. Take a deep breath. Push with all my might. *"DAD!"*

The word comes out of me as pure and loud as a bell. He stops at the sound of it, whirls around.

"COME BACK!"

He stands there, staring at me, as if he can't quite figure out what he's just heard. What has just happened. Did I look like that when I heard Mr. Thurber again after all that time?

"Pippa?" I see his mouth form my name, his hand dropping the pillowcase.

And as I run to him, I realize something about myself. Something I never thought could be possible. I have things to say. Important things. And even though they've been stuck deep down inside me for a while, I think I'm ready to make people hear them.

Chapter 44
JACK

We sit in the car for a long time after Dad gets back in again. He just slumps there behind the wheel, staring out the window. Pippa and I are both watching from the backseat. We're trying to give him space, I guess. I wonder if people feel like this after they've been hit with a stun gun: fragmented, confused. Like they've been turned inside out and upside down. For a long time, the only sound in the car is our breathing.

And then Dad starts to cry. And not just cry, but sob. But it doesn't scare me, seeing him like this. It makes me feel safe again. As if maybe the strange shell of a person he has become over the last few months has cracked and the Dad I know is finally coming out again.

Pippa and I scramble over the seat.

"I'm so, so sorry," he whispers, gathering us in his arms. "Can you ever forgive me?"

Pippa and I lock eyes over Dad's shoulder.

"We have to stop him." That was what she wrote in her notebook on the dock. *WE*. It was brave of her to include herself, but I understood it to mean that *I* was the one who had to do something before Dad went into the Sandridge bank. What in the world would Pippa do? I didn't think it would get too complicated after I refused to go in with him. Dad would have to throw in the towel when he realized he couldn't do it alone and we would go home. Or at least that was what I thought would happen. Except that it didn't. And then, although I didn't know it at the time, it really was up to Pippa.

I look at her, tucked under Dad's arm, now with her eyes closed. How was she finally able to find her voice? Where did it come from? Where has it been? Maybe the reason she stopped talking didn't have anything to do with me, after all. Maybe she just didn't have the words to tell anyone what she was feeling. Until she did again.

Dad. Her first words in almost half a year. *Come back*. And here he was.

I start to worry again on the way home. Pippa may have finally talked, but nothing's really changed. Dad still doesn't have a job, we're out of money, and the mortgage payments are just going to keep piling up. Who's to say that Dad won't slide back into feeling desperate enough to rob a bank? Why couldn't it happen again?

We're just starting down Lake Road when Dad says, "Whoa! Who is *that*? And why is he going so fast?"

I look up. It's hard to see the car coming toward us because there is so much dust flying up around it, but there's no mistaking the speed at which it's moving. Dad slows the Eldorado and pulls it over to the other side. "What in the world . . ." He squints as the car flies past us and then leans hard on the horn. "It's Nibs!" he says, leaning out the window.

Nibs brakes so hard that her back wheels skid to one side. Dirt and pebbles scatter in all directions, and the car makes a horrible screeching sound.

"Am I too late?" Her eyes are wild as she jumps out of her car and rushes toward us. "Am I too late, Sam Kendall? Did you just go do what I think you did? With your children in the car?" If she were a dragon, there would be fire coming out of her nose.

"What are you talking about?" Dad looks scared and dazed at the same time.

"I'll tell you what I'm talking about." Nibs races back to her car, grabs something inside, and races back over to Dad's side of the car. She shoves the Spider-Man and Batman masks under his nose. I can hear the crinkle of the newspaper articles inside them. "You think I don't know what these are? You think I don't know what you did with them?"

My mouth drops open. I look over at Pippa. She holds my gaze and does not blink. She doesn't say anything, but I know what she's done. And I'm glad. I'm gladder than I've been about anything in a long, long time. Because I'm not exactly sure what will happen. Or what we'll do next.

But there's one thing I do know.

Now that Nibs knows, we can't go back to where we were.

And that, I realize now, is exactly what I wanted all along.

Chapter 45
PIPPA

After Nibs stops being so mad at Dad, she takes him home. The two of them go inside her house and talk for a long, long time while Jack and I sit on the dock. The sky is gray and the cold air makes the inside of my nose prickle, but the wind is soft, so I don't mind. "You okay?" Jack asks after a while.

I nod, staring out at the water, which has turned a dark green color, the edges already slick with ice. I wonder how far Mr. Thurber has made it on his journey down South, how much longer he has to go. I miss him already, but not like before, when I was afraid I'd never see him again. Now I miss him the way I always do, impatiently, waiting for the day when I see him again.

Jack pauses for a minute, like he's hesitating. Then he says, "Can you say it? Out loud?"

I hadn't thought about saying what I said to Dad in the parking lot. It had just come out of me, like an arrow shot from a bow. I'd been scared. Desperate. It was almost as if the words had taken on a life of their own, flying out of my mouth on invisible wings. Would they come out now that I didn't feel that way anymore? "I . . ." I swallow, lick my lips, and try again. "I . . . feel okay." I glance over at my brother. "I feel okay," I say again. "Really. I do."

Jack puts his arm around me. "That's so cool," he says.

When Dad steps out Nibs' front door, he looks different. His shoulders are straight and his chin is lifted.

He sits down on the dock, right between Jack and me, and puts his arms around us. No one says anything, and for a moment it feels as if the whole lake—the water and the sky and everything between them—is holding its breath.

"I've made a mess," Dad says finally. "And it's time for me to clean it up." I watch Jack's face as he stares anxiously at Dad.

"What're you going to do?" Jack's voice is barely a whisper.

"I'm going to turn myself in."

I clutch at his sleeve, realizing what he's saying.

"You mean you're going to tell the police?" Jack's eyes are huge. "About Middlebury?"

Dad nods. "And Rutland, too. I have to, son. I won't be able to live with myself if I don't."

"But you'll go to jail!"

"I might," Dad answers. "We'll see what happens. I'm going to meet with an attorney tomorrow afternoon, and he'll go with me to the police station. If I do have to go to jail, you'll stay with Nibs. We've already talked about it."

"No!" I can feel tears rising. "I don't want you to go to jail! Please, Dad!"

He pulls back a little so that he can see both of us at the same time. "I need both of you to listen to me," he says slowly. "Something happened to me after your mother died. It's not an excuse for what I did. But it was like a part of me died with her, like I was just half a person. I wasn't thinking clearly, which is why I lost the car lot, why I invested in a ridiculous scam, and—" He pauses, running a hand through his hair. "And why I thought robbing a bank to save the house was a good idea." He wrinkles his nose, and for a split second, he looks exactly like Jack. "It took you guys to bring me back again. To realize that the part I thought had died with your mother was still very much alive. And still very much responsible as a father. If I don't own up to the mistakes I've made, I won't ever be able to look at either of you in the face again. Can you understand that?"

I think I might understand. A little. But I don't want him to go to jail. I don't want to have to miss him the way I miss Mom. I don't, I really don't.

And then Jack looks over at me. I can tell he's asking me with his eyes not to make a fuss, to let Dad do what he needs to do to make things right again. And in that moment, I realize two things. The first is that going to jail is not the same thing as dying. And the second is that no matter what happens, Jack will still be here with me.

"Pippa and I will be fine." Jack's voice wobbles. "Won't we Pip?"

I nod. And then, because both Jack and Dad are looking hopefully at me, I open my mouth.

"Yes," I say out loud. "Yes, we'll be okay."

The chairs in Mrs. Paciotti's room have been packed in so tightly that both Jack's and Dad's knees are touching the back of the chairs in front of them. Nibs keeps waving at people coming into the room and breaking into snorts whenever Miss Rhodes bends over to tell her something.

I'm a wreck. I practiced talking a little more last night, but my voice still sounds weird to me, like a stranger's. I hope it doesn't sound like that to the audience. I'm also exhausted. But I guess that comes with the territory when you stay up all night writing a paper that's due the next day. Although I couldn't have written this paper until last night anyway. Not until everything happened the way it did. Afterward, as I lay in bed, running it all through my head again, the idea for the paper came to me. Just like Nibs said it would, when I was thinking about anything except what I would write about.

"All right, everyone." Miss Rhodes stands at the front of the room behind the podium. She has a new dress on and a little yellow flower tucked behind one ear. "I think all our guests have arrived, which means we can start with our first presentation." She gives Susan a smile. "Susan? You're first."

Susan stands up, walks over to an elderly gentleman in a wheelchair, and wheels him to the front of the room, right next to the podium. "This is my great-grandfather, Arnold Biggs," she says proudly. Everyone looks at Mr. Biggs. He's dressed in an old army uniform with about twenty different medals pinned to his chest and shiny black shoes. A narrow, tent-shaped hat sits atop his head, and his hands are covered with brown spots. He gives the crowd a small wave and smiles at Susan.

Susan's speech is fantastic. By the time she's finished, everyone's in tears, including her great-grandfather. And when Miss Rhodes gives her the Spartan sash to put around him, and he kisses her on the cheek, the whole room stands up and applauds. It's a big moment. I'm so happy for her.

Five more students follow Susan, including Molly, who gives a pretty good talk about her uncle. He doesn't look like a millionaire though, in his jeans and baseball hat, and he doesn't even look like he only has one leg until he lifts his pants and shows everyone a new one that the plastics factory he owns just made for him. Raymond and George go next, and then Marissa Jones goes after them, and then it's my turn.

I walk up to the podium on trembling legs. Miss Rhodes gives my hand a squeeze and then steps aside. She gives me the same smile that she did this morning when I told her I could read the speech on my own: full of encouragement. Full of pride. I move the microphone down a little and fold over the corner of my paper. Then I look up. Molly is elbowing Susan over and over again in the ribs, but Susan is sitting on the edge of her seat, just watching. Waiting.

I look back down and swallow.

"Spartan boys had to go through very difficult things to become good soldiers," I begin. "They had to train very hard and they didn't always have good food. Sometimes they were put in dark rooms so that they would learn not to be afraid of the dark, and if they cried they would get punished. But I think the hardest thing for these boys was that they were taken away from their parents. Learning how to get through life without their mother and father was probably the most difficult thing they ever had to do."

So far, so good. My voice is getting stronger the more I talk, and some of the butterflies in my stomach are quieting down. I clear my throat. Take a deep breath.

"When our mom died of stomach cancer, it was the hardest time of our whole life. It really did feel like we were in a dark room and would never be let out again. I couldn't even talk, I was so sad. For a long time, it felt like our family was broken, and that maybe we'd never be fixed again. But my brother Jack helped put us all back together, including my dad. He stayed strong and true and loyal, just like a real Spartan warrior. Out of all of us, he was the bravest. That is why today I would like to honor him. To say thank you to my brother for everything he gave us. For helping us learn how to be a family again."

Jack comes up to the podium to get his sash as the clapping starts. Dad and Nibs are wiping tears away with balled-up tissues, and so is Miss Rhodes. I have to stand on my tiptoes to put the sash around Jack, and when I do, I can see that his ears are red. He gives me a hug. Then he looks at Miss Rhodes and points to the microphone. "By all means," she says.

Jack steps up to the podium, but not before grabbing my hand. "This is really cool," he says, "and I'm really grateful. But this sash belongs to my sister, not me. She's the real warrior here." He looks over at me and wrinkles his nose. "I didn't even know what bravery was until the last few weeks. But now I do. Bravery is being in the dark and feeling your way around until you find your way out. Bravery is losing your voice and then finding it again.

Bravery is this girl. My sister. Pippa Kendall. Spartan warrior." He takes the sash off and puts it around me.

The cheering surrounds us like water.

Outside, the sky is a brilliant blue, and in the distance, just behind the horizon, the sun is shining.

Chapter 46
JACK

"Jack." I turn around in the lunch line to see Ben. His nose is still swollen on one side, and there's something that looks like a brush burn under his left eye. "I heard Pippa's talking again," he says, shoving his hands inside his pockets. "At some presentation thing this morning?"

"Yeah." I don't know what else to say.

"That's great." Ben nods. "I'm really happy for her."

"Thanks. Me too."

I know what he's not saying. I can hear the apology and the forgiveness in his voice, just as I hope he can hear it in mine.

"Okay then. See you around?" he asks.

I want to give him a bear hug, to get him in a head-lock and knuckle his hair into a knot, to sit down across our table so that we can catch up on everything we've missed over the last six months. I want to do this, but I won't. Not today.

But soon.

Very soon.

I lift my hand as he walks away. "See you around, Ben."

─────────────────────────────

"Thanks for saving me a seat," Shelby says, sliding in next to me. "I heard Pippa's presentation was a big hit."

"It was great." I take a big bite of mashed potatoes, but they're hard to swallow. I can't get Dad off my mind, the way he hugged me so tightly when he said good-bye after Pippa's presentation, the look in his eyes as he waved from the car. His meeting with his attorney was at 11:30. It's 12:15 now. I wonder if they're done. If they're on their way down to the police station.

"She talked to me a little bit about it this morning," Shelby says. "On the bus, remember?"

I think back, remember how wide Shelby's eyes got when Pippa slid in the seat behind her and said "Good morning," but I don't recall her saying anything else.

"What'd she say?"

"She was telling me about the speech." Shelby's looking at me funny. "You were right there. Didn't you hear her?"

I look down at my meatloaf. The truth is, while Shelby was listening to Pippa this morning, I was thinking about Mom. About how she'd told me to do whatever it took because family was everything, and how I'd messed up what she'd meant by that. Whatever it took didn't mean doing anything to keep us together. It meant doing the right thing, no matter how hard it was, just like Dad was going to do this afternoon when he went down to talk to his attorney about what he'd done. It meant not giving up on each other. Finding new ways to solve old problems. Doing what we needed to do to get back to the place where we'd been so that we could get to the place we needed to go. I'm not sure how Dad forgot this. Or if he ever knew it at all. But maybe that doesn't matter. Maybe the only thing that really matters is that we're all still trying.

"I missed it," I say now. "I was thinking about my Mom."

Shelby smiles at me. "Guess what?"

"What?"

"I got a phone call this morning."

I look up. "From who?"

"My mom."

"You did?"

She nods, taking an enormous bite of potatoes. "She's feeling so much better. She's coming up in two weeks."

Something plummets in the bottom of my stomach. "To take you back to Texas?"

"No." Shelby shakes her head. "Just to visit. I'm going to stay here for the rest of the year and she'll visit when she can. It's the best thing right now. For both of us, I think."

"That's great, Shelby." I reach down for her hand and squeeze it hard inside my mine. "I'm really happy for you."

"Thanks," she says, beaming. "I am too."

APRIL

Chapter 47
PIPPA

"You sure you'll be okay if I hang out at Ben's this afternoon?" It's April, and Jack takes my hand as we make our way across the middle school parking lot and into the high school. "It's really fine if you want me to stay. I mean it."

"No, I'm fine." I twist out of his grip as we enter the building; it's full of teenagers, and I don't need any of them thinking I'm some kind of a baby. With its enormous glass windows and vaulted ceilings, the high school always makes me think of some kind of outer space museum. Kids of every shape and size swarm around us. A girl in tight blue jeans and a yellow gingham shirt is holding a boy's hand just by the pinky finger, and two guys off to the right are laughing and pushing each other against the wall. It's hard to believe Jack will go to school here in just over a year. And then me.

"You're sure?" Jack asks again.

"*Yes*," I repeat. "Geez, Jack, you're starting to sound like Mom."

The comment catches both of us off guard, mostly because I've never said anything like that before, and because it's true—Mom used to fret exactly like this—but I'd forgotten it until now. For a split second, our eyes meet, and then we both smile.

"Not a bad thing," he says finally, weaving me in and around another cluster of high school kids. "Okay, here we are."

Inside her classroom, Nibs is wrapping her green scarf around her neck, even though it is sixty degrees outside, and shoving papers inside a small satchel. "Hello, my darlings," she says. "You're right on time. Ready to go?"

"I'm catching a ride home with Ben," Jack says. "Remember?"

"Of course I remember," Nibs says, looking at him fondly. "You're going fishing, right?"

"Right." Jack reaches over and squeezes my hand. "I'll catch one just for you, Pip," he says, giving me a wink. "I'll bring it home and gut it right on the deck, eyeballs and everything . . ."

"Bye!" I start laughing as I push him out of the room, then stand and watch as he races back down the hall. Four months ago, he would have never done such a thing. The first few weeks after Dad got sentenced to jail for a year, Jack barely let me go to the bathroom without him. It didn't matter that Nibs was the one in charge and that he was her responsibility now just as much as I was. He guarded me like a hawk, like a mother bear watching her cub. He still does, honestly, although he's loosened up a little, thank goodness. Now, even when we go visit Dad on weekends, he doesn't make me sit in the back of the car with him or hold his hand the whole time we're in the visiting room.

"You ready to get dirty?" Nibs puts her arm around me as we walk out of her room. "I've got a whole garden just waiting to be dug up this afternoon. What say we put on a pair of overalls, get ourselves nice and filthy, and then have a cookout for dinner?"

"Can Shelby come?"

"Of course she can come." Nibs nods toward her car. "Go ask her yourself."

Shelby is leaning against Nibs' car, the way she always is every afternoon at this time. She waves as I run to her, and it occurs to me that maybe this is how life works sometimes: A sudden stumble interrupts the regular walk of your life. Maybe even throws you off course. But then it gradually picks up again, and slowly, finally, you settle into a new pace. A new routine. And it's the new routine that can be tricky. You have to figure out different rules, navigate new terrain, look in different mirrors if you want to see yourself again. But it's not impossible if you have the right people to do it with. Having the right people with you makes all the difference.

Having the right people with you, as Mom would say, is everything.

Acknowledgments

First thanks goes to my Spartan warrior of an agent, Stacey Glick, whose enthusiasm and encouragement remain an unfailing source of inspiration. My brilliant editor, Jenne Abramowitz, takes my books from chrysalis to butterfly and then cheers as they take flight. I couldn't do it without you, friend. Thank you to all the amazingly creative people at Scholastic, for the beautiful book cover and for everything you've done to bring this one out into the world. Final thanks to my children, who continue to redefine the word *love* for me, each and every day.